THRUST

THE ALPHA ESCORT SERIES

SYBIL BARTEL

Books by Sybil Bartel

The Alpha Escort Series
THRUST
ROUGH
GRIND

The Uncompromising Series
TALON
NEIL
ANDRÉ
BENNETT
CALLAN

The Alpha Bodyguard Series
SCANDALOUS
MERCILESS
RECKLESS
RUTHLESS
FEARLESS
CALLOUS
RELENTLESS

The Alpha Antihero Series
HARD LIMIT
HARD JUSTICE
HARD SIN

The Unchecked Series
IMPOSSIBLE PROMISE
IMPOSSIBLE CHOICE

IMPOSSIBLE END

The Rock Harder Series
NO APOLOGIES

Join Sybil Bartel's Mailing List to get the news first on her upcoming releases, giveaways and exclusive excerpts! You'll also get a FREE book for joining!

THRUST

Alex

I know the game. I know the angle. I know how to make you beg.

My hands on your body, my mouth hovering over yours—I'll tell you everything you want to hear. Ten inches of real estate never felt so good.

But don't take my word for it. My client list is long and my motto is short—one single thrust and you're mine. I'm not good at what I do, I'm fantastic. But satisfaction doesn't come cheap. So open your wallet and prepare to forget your name. I'm about to ruin you for any other man.

One single thrust and you're mine.

DEDICATION

Dad, please don't read this book.

ONE

Alex

"AH, AH, AH." I PULLED HER HAIR JUST ENOUGH to get her red lips away from my dick. "You know the rules."

"*Please*?" she begged, pouting.

Damn, she made it too easy. I half smiled and stroked myself. "You wanna wrap your mouth around this?" Fake tits, tight ass, she was hot for a cougar, but that wasn't what was making my dick hard. Another grand on the table was doing that all on its own.

"Yes," she hissed huskily.

My clients were all the same. They got off on the idea of blowing a male escort like they could do it better than I'd ever had it. And I was only too happy to capitalize on that. "You wanna suck me off, beautiful?" I frowned and stroked harder, as if I were close. "Because you're gonna have to pay for it."

On her knees, she practically trembled. "Whatever it costs."

Music to my ears. I shoved the tip of my dick into her hot mouth. "Then show me what you got."

She sucked. Eagerly. I threw my head back and groaned like it was the best fucking blowjob ever.

A half hour later, I filled the second condom and pulled out. "Damn, gorgeous, you've got me so worn out, I need to go home and sleep for a week." I glanced at the clock. I had another client in forty. "You were fucking incredible." She was decent. I slapped her ass so I didn't have to kiss her.

She giggled like a schoolgirl and batted her eyelashes. "You weren't so bad yourself."

I smirked. She'd be texting me before the night was out to schedule another session. "How do you wanna settle up?" I tied off the condom and slipped it into my pocket as I pulled my pants up. Rule number one—never leave behind any evidence.

Naked except for her heels, she got off the bed and sauntered to her purse. "How much?"

"Four grand." I smiled like I was checking her out.

"Four?"

I took two strides and tipped her chin. "Two rounds and oral. You want a third? I just got hard watching that ass of yours." I could fit in another quickie before my next appointment.

She smiled coyly. "Maybe next time."

I held back my laugh, just barely. I was hung as hell. If she wasn't sore from all that pounding, my name wasn't Alex Vega. "You know where to find me." I dropped her chin. "Cash or credit?"

She handed me her card and I swiped it through the small credit card reader attached to my cell phone. "Need me to text you a receipt?"

She smiled. "Receipt?"

"Deep tissue massage." I was legit as fuck. I'd even gotten the damn massage therapist license. "Medical expense. You can deduct it on your taxes." I winked. "You're welcome."

She shook her head but she looked amused. The card went through and I got dressed ASAP. Rule number two—never stick around—unless they pay you.

"So...." She twirled her hair like she was twelve. "What are you doing Saturday night? I'm looking for a date to this fundraiser that's for—"

I was already shaking my head. "Sorry, babe. I don't do show and tell. Strictly bedroom scenes. But text me after if you're bored." I shot her my money smile and buckled my Ferragamo belt, then threw on the jacket of my custom-tailored suit. Stepping into my loafers sans socks, I was out. "Later, gorgeous." Three steps backward, a wink for good measure and I turned. I couldn't hit the door fast enough.

On the elevator ride to the lobby, I checked my messages, scheduled three more clients and pulled up my E-Trade account balance. Nothing got me hard like seven digits in a row. It was already a twenty-grand week and I hadn't even hit the weekend.

I palmed a hundred and shook hands with the concierge on my way out. Another hundred and the valet had my McLaren 570S waiting. I slid behind the wheel of my silver beauty and hit the gas. This car was a fucking orgasm on steroids.

Weaving in and out of Miami's traffic, I made it to my penthouse on Collins Avenue in record time and rushed through a shower and a change. Fresh suit, pressed dress shirt, I picked out a new belt and shoes. Then I used the cologne I remembered my client saying she liked because it was all in the details. A half hour later, I was pulling up to the W in South Beach.

I checked the room number one of my regulars had

texted me and greeted a valet I hadn't seen before. "You're new."

"Yes, sir. Checking in?"

Blond hair cut with a buzzer, he couldn't have been much younger than me. A few years ago, I *was* him. Different uniform, but the end result was the same—I was watching life from the sidelines and fucking for free.

"Meeting friends." I tipped my chin at my baby. "Keep her close and there'll be something in it for you." I couldn't remember the last time I'd fucked for free.

The valet kid stood taller because in this town, money and fast cars talked. "Yes, sir. Of course, sir."

I slapped him on the shoulder. "Excellent. Two hours." Fucker better not nut himself on my leather seats.

"Two hours," he repeated, practically drooling as he got behind the wheel.

I took the elevator to the fourteenth floor and strode to the room like I was a king. Goddamn, a flush bank account and a ten-inch cock were a winning combination.

I knocked and a few seconds later, Irina opened the door. Tall, blonde and model thin, she'd been one of my first clients and I'd seen her every week since.

"Hey, baby." I stepped in and kicked the door shut behind me. Gripping two handfuls of her hair because that's what she liked, I cocked my head and looked down at her like I gave a shit. "You wait for me this week?"

"*Alex*," she said breathlessly in her Russian accent. "I always wait for you."

"Right answer." I kissed her.

Hot and hard, I bit her bottom lip and aggressively took control. She was the only client I ever kissed anymore. I'd learned after I'd already broken the rules with her that kissing clients was a recipe for disaster. They got attached, every damn time. Except Irina. I couldn't tell if she just didn't give a shit or if she was too practical to fall for a guy. Either way, she sucked my dick like a pro, so I didn't give two fucks about breaking the rules and swapping tongues with her. I did it because I could. But if I ever stopped to think about it, which I absolutely didn't, I'd be a fucking pussy and say I missed kissing a hot chick.

I stroked my tongue deep, sucked hers into my mouth, and she melted into me. I cupped her ass and squeezed, but then I yanked her hair back. "Hey." I scanned her body. "You lose more weight?" I didn't mind models, but Irina was thin to begin with and I had a steel-trap memory. She'd definitely had more substance the last time we were together.

Her disinterested expression washed over her features and she sighed. "I am stressed."

Fucking familiarity threw me and I asked why before I could rein it in. "About?"

"The Third is divorcing me." She strolled through the suite like a lazy cat and went straight for the balcony and a glass of wine she had waiting. "Want some?" She held her glass up.

I knew she was married to some prick twice her age who came from old money but I'd never asked details. She called him the Third since he was one, and she claimed he knew we fucked because he stopped being able to get it up long ago. I didn't know how much was truth or bullshit, but I suspected it was all true. Irina couldn't be bothered to lie. She didn't have to. She was fucking loaded and gave even less of a shit about decorum than I did.

I took the glass from her hand and set it back on the table. "I'm ordering food, then we'll talk."

She sank down onto the padded chair on the balcony and threw a leg over the arm. "Whatever."

I went inside, ordered steak, fish and a pasta entrée from room service because I didn't know what the hell she ate. I added a bottle of Jack, a bucket of ice and told them to throw in two desserts. I kicked off my shoes, stripped out of my jacket and shirt and made my way back to the balcony.

With her head back and her hair falling down the back of the chair, she looked young as hell but I didn't know how old she was. Her body was that of a twenty-year-old but the dead look in her eyes made her seem fifty.

"Get up," I ordered.

She glared at me then got up real slow, as if she had all the time in the world.

I smirked and slapped her ass. "Brat." I sat in the chair she'd just vacated. "Now sit." I held an arm out.

She lounged across my lap. Her legs were over the side of the chair like before, but her head was now resting on my shoulder. She curled toward me and placed a hand on the abs I worked my ass off in the gym for. "I don't want to talk. I want to fuck."

My dick hardened because it knew just what her pussy felt like. "After you eat. Why's the Third divorcing you?" I didn't give a shit why, I just didn't want the steady income to stop.

She traced a finger down my stomach, toying with me. "He says I am not happy."

"He's met you, right?"

She slapped my stomach. "Don't be an ass."

I laughed but I wasn't entirely kidding. "Come on, you

6

know I'm playing but he's not that far off. What do you ever get excited about?"

"Your cock."

I grinned and thrust my hips up just to fuck with her. "Besides that."

"Nothing."

Except she didn't say it on a sigh like she did when she was being her usual disinterested self. Her voice went quiet and the single word was soft and low like she was confessing. My shoulders dropped and I leaned my head back.

Shit.

I never thought I'd have to deal with this from her. "I'm not for keeps, Irina." I didn't do attachments, or any other shit that tied you to another human being.

She got even quieter. "I know."

"You sure?" Damn it, I didn't want to lose a steady client but I also didn't fuck clingers or stalkers.

"Yes, yes," she huffed. "I know. No boyfriend, no husband, just fucking."

"And paying," I reminded her.

The side of her mouth tipped up in a rare smile.

I smiled back. "Good, now that we got that settled, you'll eat some damn food so I can enjoy fucking you."

"You will like it anyway."

She was right. She was one of the few clients I enjoyed fucking just for the sex. "You'll like it more." I grinned as a knock sounded on the door. "Up you go." I lifted her off my lap and went to meet room service. Two strides before the door, I felt it.

I glanced over my shoulder.

Sure enough, she was watching me like an abandoned puppy.

Fuck.

TWO

Olivia

I BLINKED. THEN I BLINKED AGAIN. I COULDN'T STOP IT, MY hand went up in the universal you've-got-to-be-kidding-me gesture. "Okay, wait. You're saying the piece can't be hung here because the wall is *what*?"

The greasy-haired artist shook his head like a pendulum on speed as he stared at his feet and walked in a circle. "It's not grounded, man. It's just not grounded. This wall, it's no good." He stopped and suddenly threw his arms up and tilted his head back like he'd just discovered the sun. "It needs to breathe."

Oh my God. I pretended to study the painting that was a mess of colors with shit brown dripping off the bottom half like he'd dunked it in an overflowing toilet. "It looks pretty grounded to me."

His arms went down and he cocked his head. "You think so?"

I nodded enthusiastically. "Oh yeah, totally." *Not.*

He scratched his beard. "Maybe it needs more effervescence. You know, to match the space?"

I wanted to rip my hair out and trust me, that was a big fucking deal. I'd spent a week's income on getting my hair cut and styled for this fundraiser. "I think we're good, Franklin. The opening is tomorrow and this piece will be the star of the show." I didn't know what painting would be the star of the show and I didn't care. The only thing I knew about art was that rich people paid top dollar for trendy shit and whacked-out artists like this guy made more on one painting than I did in a year.

Franklin abruptly stepped back and made a sweeping motion with his hands that was directed at the baseboard. "Can we, you know, anchor this wall somehow?"

"Anchor it?" *It's a wall.*

"Yeah, something heavy—to keep it down?" He peered at me, completely serious.

"We're twenty-five stories up and the wall is attached to the floor. Pretty sure it's not going anywhere."

"Sandbags?"

I pressed my lips together and shook my head. "Sorry, fresh out." We were in Miami Beach in a penthouse, for Christ's sake.

He snapped his fingers. "Potatoes! Like those sacks, man. The big ones!"

"Sorry, building codes—this space isn't zoned for commercial food service." I didn't know what it was zoned for. All I knew, my best friend had hooked me up. He was in construction and this penthouse was one of his current projects. The floors were still bare concrete and the walls were framed and drywalled, but nothing else had been done. Floor-to-ceiling windows, recessed lighting everywhere, it was a perfect spot to showcase the eleven artists I'd painstakingly convinced to participate in my fundraiser for Canine Watch.

SYBIL BARTEL

"It needs *something*, man."

I sighed. "You do realize I'm a woman?"

His head popped up and he looked at me funny. "What?"

"You're familiar with them?" I didn't know why I was wasting my time.

His face scrunched up. "Who?"

"Women." Was I speaking French?

He snapped his fingers. "Yeah, yeah, totally. You're that dog chick."

Kill me now. "Dog chick?"

"You like, give dogs to people with bad juju."

Seriously? He was equating PTSD with *juju*? "How old are you?"

"Twenty-five."

"And you say *juju*?" I didn't even bother to explain the difference between that and PTSD. He looked like he was a decade into his brain-altering narcotics long-term plan and nothing I said was going to stick.

He frowned. "I did?"

I bit the inside of my cheek so I didn't scream. "Mm-hmm."

His smile was wide. "Cool."

I sucked in a breath and wiped my expression clean. "So we're good? You're comfortable now? Because I have to do a walk-through with the fire marshal. You know...," I held my breath and leaned toward him, "To make sure there's nothing *illegal* here," I stage-whispered.

His smile dropped and his hand went to his pocket. He grabbed it from the outside like he needed to make sure something was still there. "Yeah, yeah, I feel you. I'm cool."

I shuffled him toward the elevator. "Great, thanks so

10

much. I can't wait for tomorrow night. Make sure you're here by nine. You can mingle with all the buyers, talk to them, tell them your inspiration." I jabbed the call button and the doors to the dedicated elevator slid right open. Hoping I didn't catch some flesh-eating virus from his rank clothes, I pushed Franklin inside. "See you tomorrow." The doors shut and I exhaled.

"Fire marshal?"

My hand flew to my chest and I spun. "Shit, Jesse, you scared me."

The lines in the corners of his big brown eyes crinkled and his perfect smile lit up his face. "I thought you were going to lose it when he said he wanted a sack of potatoes."

"Oh my God," I groaned. "Don't remind me." I mentally added *heavy object* to my to-do list because despite me pushing Franklin out, I didn't want any problems tomorrow night. If he wanted something leaning on the wall under his painting, I was sure I could come up with at least a sack of dirty laundry.

Jesse chuckled. "How much weed do you think he smokes in a day?" He glanced down as he placed his hammer back in his tool belt and his messy blond hair fell over one eye. When he looked up, he flipped his head and my stomach fluttered.

I smirked to hide my doe eyes. "I don't know but I bet it's in direct correlation to how much he gets paid for a painting." I nodded at the toilet water one. "And that one has an opening bid of twenty-five grand."

Jesse's eyes went wide. "You've got to be kidding me." He stared at the canvas that was a bigger disaster than the artist himself. "For a painting that looks like it just messed itself?"

I smiled. Neither of us knew shit about art. "Yep. And

let's hope it goes for double that, because fifty percent of every sale goes to the charity."

Jesse glanced back at me and the softness in his expression was one I used to stay awake nights fantasizing about, until he got a girlfriend.

"Not just any charity, *your* charity."

I nodded like it was no big deal but my heart swelled with pride. "Well, someone had to do something."

"And that someone was you." He put his arm around my shoulders like he'd done thousands of times before. "Proud of you, Liv."

I leaned my head into his chest for just a moment and breathed him in. Soap and construction dust and the scent that'd grown from teenager to man. Jesse Emerson had been my best friend since ninth grade. "Thanks, Jess. I just hope tomorrow pulls in the numbers I need to keep afloat." I'd invested every penny I had and if tomorrow didn't bring in enough money, I'd be homeless within a week. But more, I'd be a failure at the one thing I swore I'd never fail at again.

"It's going to be great. You'll see. How many invites did you send out?"

Invites, ads, flyers, I'd even put posters up at all the nearby pet stores and vet offices. Most of those places wouldn't net me a buyer who could afford the price of a painting, but it didn't matter, I was trying to create a buzz. I wanted media coverage and the more people who showed up tomorrow, the more it would drive up the prices with the serious bidders. At least, that was my theory. I'd never actually done a fundraiser before. "A few hundred."

Jesse squeezed my shoulder then released me. "Well, Jennifer and I will be here."

Jennifer and Jesse. I even hated how their names matched. "Great, thanks. That means a lot." I meant it, I swear I did, but it still kinda sucked saying it.

"No problem. And you're all set, every picture is hung."

"You're the best, seriously. I couldn't have pulled this together without you." I went on tiptoe and hugged him. "I know how busy with work you are and transitioning to the northern office." My heart broke just saying it. Minus the time he was deployed, Jesse and I had lived in the same city since we were kids. He was a construction project manager for a firm that built high-rises in Miami, which was how I was able to use this space for the show. But his boss, who ran operations in northern Florida, decided to relocate to Miami. He asked Jesse to take over the Orlando office. I was super proud of him, but I selfishly didn't want him to move.

He hugged me back hard then pulled away. "Hey, you're not getting rid of me yet. I still have a couple more weeks before I move."

"How'd Jennifer take the news?" The last time we'd spoken about Jesse moving, I was shocked to find out he hadn't told his girlfriend.

His face clouded over. "I'll tell her soon."

If it was any other night besides the one before my fundraiser, I would've paid attention to the tight set of his jaw or asked what he was waiting for. Jennifer would jump at the chance to relocate with him. Any woman would. Jesse was the perfect catch. Gorgeous, kind, considerate, and he made great money. But I didn't ask. "So, see you tomorrow night?"

He stared at me a second then shook his head like he was shaking away a thought and smiled. "Yep. Call me if Mr. Potato Sack needs a good ass kicking."

I laughed. Jesse was a lot of things, but he wasn't an ass kicker. He'd talk you down and reason it out. Despite his tall frame and solid muscles that came from years of hard manual labor, he wasn't a fighter. "Get out of here before I find something else for you to do, like fill sandbags."

He smiled briefly then his expression turned serious. "Your brother would've been proud of you." He kissed my cheek and walked to the elevator like he hadn't just gutted me. "Night, Liv."

I stared at the elevator long after the doors closed.

My brother wouldn't have been proud of me. I'd let him die.

THREE

Alex

I TOOK THE BRUNETTE BY THE HAIR. "WHAT'S MY NAME?"

"A-A-A-Alex."

"What?" I barked.

"Alex," she whimpered.

I didn't give a fuck what she called me. "Say it again," I bit out even louder.

"Alex!"

"Who controls you?"

"You do."

"Who makes you come?" Technically, she made herself come. I never actually touched her beyond pulling her hair or spanking her ass.

"You do."

I bent to her ear. "Never fucking forget it." I released her as if I was disgusted with her, but I couldn't care less. She paid cash at the beginning of every session and her script was always the same. "Get in the fucking shower. I'm done with you."

She scrambled on her hands and knees as if she were my sub and I'd told her to crawl, but she had no fucking clue what a real sub was. Most of my clients didn't. They read that book, decided they wanted a little dominance, then I'd get a call. I was bossy as fuck, I'd make them come a few times, then I'd take their money. But true BDSM? Not my gig.

The second I heard the shower turn on, I was out. Easiest three grand I'd make all week. But the thought didn't turn me on. I didn't even check my account or look at my schedule for next week as I walked out of the hotel.

For the past two days, all I'd been thinking about was the look on Irina's face when I'd told her we were done. I'd expected her I-don't-give-a-fuck attitude but all I'd gotten was sad eyes and silence. That only reaffirmed my decision to get rid of her before she became a problem, but the incident kept replaying in my head.

I didn't give a shit that I wasn't going to see her again. I wasn't even going to miss her. Except I kept thinking I should feel something for a client I'd fucked every week for three years, but I didn't. The only thing I felt, when I wasn't being apathetic as hell, was relief. And that was fucking with my head.

I drove home, showered, changed and forced myself to focus on my next client. Trina Howards. Ten grand for two hours at some fucking charity event for veterans. The irony wasn't lost on me. The Marines had given me a backbone and taught me how to be commanding as fuck. I'd walked away when my service was up without looking back once, but here I was going to a fundraiser for vets when I'd sworn I'd never meet a client outside the bedroom. I blamed the loss of income from dumping Irina on my shit decision to agree to this event, but it was bullshit.

I had a waiting list as long as my cock. I could've pulled a few names and made more money fucking than ten grand for a charity event. But I didn't. I was driving to a half-finished penthouse to look at paintings because I wasn't about to admit that after three years of screwing my way through Miami's wealthiest women, I was burnt out.

I pulled up to a valet that was clearly set up for tonight and cursed. If my car got scratched, I was charging Trina triple.

The valet opened my door and I gave the zit-faced kid a once-over. "You ever driven a McLaren before?"

"Yes, sir."

"I want her left in front, not parked close to anyone else and if shit isn't fucked-up when I come back, I'll tip accordingly. Do we understand each other?"

"Absolutely, sir." He nodded toward a black Navigator with the windows tinted out. "I think your date is waiting. She said you drive a McLaren."

Christ. "Thanks." I walked to the Lincoln and stood a few feet from the back door. Half smile, all attitude, I crossed my arms.

Trina didn't even wait for her driver to open the door. She burst out of the SUV looking like she'd already had a few. "Alex!"

Fuck me. She'd had more than a few. "Trina."

"*Hellooo*," she cooed, stumbling in her heels.

I didn't reach for her, or smile. "You start without me?"

She teetered over and grasped my arms as she leaned into me. "Yes, but…." She breathed alcohol breath all over me and turned serious. "Do you know what it's like to get all prettied up then wait for a man you're *paying* to pretend to like you? My self-esteem *needed* that drink, or three." She nodded theatrically.

"Babe, you're hot." It wasn't a lie. Money bought all sorts of shit, like personal trainers and plastic surgery.

"You think so?"

Damn, if I was going to play therapist, I needed to up my rates. "Want in on a little secret?"

"Okay." She bit her lip.

I leaned down to her ear and lowered my voice. "Guys get off on a confident woman."

Her shoulders squared and she lifted her chin. "You're going to *love* fucking me later."

"You'll love it more." Guaranteed.

Throaty and honest, she laughed. "You're right."

I shook my head but that time, my half smile was real. "Let's go look at your art." With a hand on her back, I led her into the lobby and we were directed to the penthouse's elevator.

Once we were alone inside the elevator, she copped a feel. "How long do we have to stay?"

I didn't bother pointing out this was her gig. Women didn't pay me to be a passive fuck. My clients wanted alpha and I didn't know any other way. "You're going to look at every piece." I pulled her hand off my dick and held it away from my body. "Pretend to deliberate over a couple then buy three of the most expensive ones." I pushed her against the wall and leaned close but I stopped just short of my body touching hers. "Then I'll take you to the Setai and fuck you sober." I tightened my grip on her hand. "But only if you're a good girl and keep your hands to yourself." I narrowed my eyes. "Can you manage that?" I wasn't stupid enough to let a client grope me in public. "Otherwise, I'm out."

"Ohhh, playing hard to get?" She smiled but it was slightly off. "Don't forget I'm paying you."

I let my gaze drift over her mouth, her fake double D's and

her narrow waist. Then I lingered at the juncture of her thighs. It took two seconds to make her squirm. "Do you know why I'm the best?" I asked quietly.

Every ounce of indignation left her voice. "No."

I drew a single finger up the outside of her thigh and lifted the hem of her dress a few inches. "Because not only do I know how to make you come so hard it hurts." I met her hungry gaze and dropped my voice as I enunciated each word. "I don't need you." I abruptly stepped back and the elevator doors slid open. "Ready?"

She shivered and pressed her legs together. "Oh, you're good."

"Like I said, the best." I guided her out of the elevator with a hand at her back.

"You're a cocky little—"

I gripped her nape and stopped her. "I assure you, there is nothing *little* about me." I dropped my hand, forced an amused smile and we walked into the party.

It was like every other bullshit charity event. Posers, older women in heels, money and a solid display of Botox—with one exception.

Her ass was fucking perfect.

Small waist that swelled into round hips and an honest-to-God heart-shaped ass. The whole package was wrapped in a tight black dress, fuck-me heels and legs that went on for days.

Damn.

"Mingle, babe. I'm getting us drinks." I didn't give Trina time to answer. I was already making my way toward those sexy curves because I needed to see the face attached to that body.

I walked right up behind her and leaned toward her ear. No perfume. Just soap, shampoo, and pure intoxicating woman. "Buy you a drink, beautiful?" Anticipation made my mouth water as I waited for her to turn around.

Jesus Christ.

She was fucking gorgeous. Deep blue eyes, dark brown silky hair pinned up, her tits matched the luscious swell of her hips and her scowl made my dick come to life.

"It's an open bar," she said dryly.

Fuck me. A grin spread across my face like it was Christmas morning. Goddamn, I loved a challenge. "Did I say here?" I winked.

She forced a smile. "Check out the paintings. There are plenty left to bid on, Mr....? I'm sorry, I didn't catch your name."

"I didn't introduce myself." Five minutes alone with her. That's all I needed to turn her into a client. But the second I thought it, my smile faltered.

"Right. Well, enjoy your evening." She pivoted and walked away.

Sucker punched, my eyes glued to that ass, I didn't notice Trina come up.

Her hand wrapped around my arm like a vise grip. "Where are our drinks?"

Forcing myself to look away from the brunette, I glanced pointedly at Trina's hand. "Rules, babe," I warned.

She dropped her arm but pushed her fake tits against me and smiled. "Better?"

Ten grand, I reminded myself. "Wine?"

"I have a bottle at my place," she flirted.

Christ. "Two choices. The Setai or another hotel." If she kept this up, I was dropping her too.

THRUST

She pushed her bottom lip out. "But the wine here is probably warm."

"You're not here to drink. Which paintings did you pick?" I scanned the crowd.

"I don't need any new art." She pouted. "I'm ready to go."

Graceful, with a reserved smile, the brunette moved from one couple to another. I thought about bagging Trina's ten grand and ushering her back to her driver but quickly dismissed the idea. I wasn't walking out of here until I at least knew the brunette's name.

I glanced at Trina. "You can find at least one."

"Are you going to help me pick it out?" She batted her eyelashes.

Someone needed to tell women everywhere they should never do that. "You going to pay me to be your art consultant?"

She dropped the baby voice. "Just get me a drink."

This was why I never took my services outside the bedroom.

FOUR

Olivia

I SNUCK INTO THE BACK HALLWAY AND LEANED AGAINST the wall. Hands shaking, I pulled up the app that was tracking all the bids. Two swipes and I squeezed my eyes shut for a moment as it loaded the totals. *Please, please, please* let this happen.

"Taking a breather?"

My eyes popped open and I gasped when I saw the numbers before I lifted my head toward the sexy male voice.

Incredibly tall, too many muscles and way too gorgeous to be real, the guy who'd tried to hit on me earlier lifted his eyebrows. "Was it something I said?"

His suit was custom, his attitude was one-hundred percent douche and his smile said he owned it. "You wish." I looked back down at my phone and refrained from pumping my fist in the air. Triple, *triple* my minimum need and the bidding wasn't set to close for another hour.

"I don't have to wish, gorgeous. I get what I want, always."

I scrolled on my phone to double-check all the bids to make sure I wasn't dreaming. "Good for you." Holy shit. I could triple the number of animals I took in to train. *I could hire someone to help me.*

"Your boyfriend sexting you?"

I glanced up. Okay, he was hot as hell, I'd give him that. Piercing blue eyes, black hair, perfectly chiseled features, and he wore his suit and his attitude, it didn't wear him. But I was spot-on with my earlier assessment. He was a total douche and I was done pretending to be polite. He wasn't going to buy anything. He'd been too busy keeping his date's hands off him to even look at any of the paintings. "Yeah, and if you don't mind, I'd like a little privacy so I can get off."

Brilliant and consuming, he smiled. It would've made my heart flutter if I went for his type, which I didn't. Ever.

He tipped his drink at me then took a sip. "By all means, don't let me stop you." His shoulder hit the wall and he sank a hand into his pocket like he was settling in to watch a show.

"Shouldn't you get back to your girlfriend?" The woman he'd walked in with looked twice his age, but hell, who was I to judge? Maybe he liked cougars.

"Not my girlfriend." He took another sip.

"Good luck with that." When his date hadn't been pawing him, she'd been eye-fucking him. I took a step but he pushed off the wall and blocked me.

Using the hand that was holding his drink, he skimmed the backs of his fingers down the length of my arm. "Don't you need to take care of something?" His lips curved mischievously as he looked pointedly between my legs, tipped the glass to his mouth and drew in a few ice cubes. His jaw shifted and the brilliant smile was back. "Or maybe you need me to cool you down."

Oh my God. "Does that actually work for you?"

He ran his tongue over his top lip. "Does what work?"

His voice was pure innocence but his narrowed, knowing eyes were all attitude.

"If you actually think a woman gets off on having ice shoved up her—whatever, I feel sorry for you."

"I don't think women like it, I *know* they do. And just so we're clear, yes, you'd love it. Your body, my mouth and this glass of ice." He shook the tumbler. "Five minutes and I'll make you come. Twice." He winked. "Guaranteed or your money back."

"*Olivia.*" Jesse rounded the corner and gave the douche a once-over then looked at me. "You okay?"

"Yeah, I'm fine." Seriously, ice? *Down there*? Who the hell did this guy think he was? And why was I even thinking about it? I hated the douche's cocky attitude and worse, I'd suddenly become aware of exactly how long it'd been since I'd screwed around with anyone.

Jesse took my hand. "I think you're needed out front."

I mentally shook away all thoughts about ice and tried to focus on something, anything, besides douche's stupid, brilliant smile. "Okay." I should ask Jesse where Jennifer was. He'd shown up tonight solo and looking out of sorts but I'd been too busy to talk to him about it.

The douche casually sized Jesse up then raised an eyebrow at me. "The boyfriend?" He smiled like we shared a secret.

Jesse glared at him. "Do I know you?"

The douche glanced at our joined hands and smirked. "Not the boyfriend." He took another ice cube into his mouth and crunched down on it like he didn't give a fuck about Jesse or his question.

If I had half a brain, I would've told myself I didn't find his attitude at all attractive. I also would've told myself not to compare his perfectly draped suit to Jesse's rumpled jacket. "Let's go. I have to check on the artists." I tugged on Jesse's hand and took a step.

"Good night, *Olivia*." Smooth and calculated, the douche said my name like he knew me intimately. "Thanks for the show, gorgeous."

With a hatred in his eyes I'd never seen, Jesse glared at the dude, and I yanked him down the hallway. "Come on."

The anger didn't recede from his features but he followed me. "Do you know who that is?"

"No. Where's Jennifer?"

His gaze drifted to the front door of the penthouse and he dropped my hand as two men approached.

One was huge and menacing and the other was blond and grinning. The blond raked his gaze over my dress and his whole face lit up with mischief. "Damn, Fixer, you didn't tell me your girlfriend was hot." He shook hands with Jesse as he slapped him on the back but his bright, green-eyed gaze didn't leave mine. "Hey, darlin'."

"Because she's not my girlfriend. Olivia, this is Talon. Talon, this is my friend Olivia. She's the event organizer and the charity is hers." Jesse tipped his chin at the taller guy. "Boss."

Talon laughed and more than a few heads turned because it was that infectious. "Then I'd say you picked the wrong girlfriend." He held his arm out as he stepped toward me. "Come here, gorgeous, gimme some love."

"Talon," Jesse warned, but it was too late.

Talon had already pulled me into a bear hug. He smelled like the beach and coconuts, and his presence was so commanding and his arms so strong that I fell into his hug as if we were long-lost friends. "Don't mind Fixer, darlin'. He's just jealous because I'm better lookin'." Talon released me.

"Fixer?"

Jesse sighed. "He nicknames everyone."

Talon grinned. "Yeah, Fixer. You know, mender, builder, carpenter. He's always tryin' to fix shit and since Jesus's name was already taken"—he shrugged—"Fixer it was."

Jesse shook his head and glanced at the other man. "This is Neil Christensen. The owner of NC Construction and my boss."

Neil tipped his chin and studied me like he could see right through me. Jesse had told me he was ex-Danish Military Special Forces and he'd said he was tall, but he didn't tell me he was six and half feet of menacing muscle with eyes the color of ice. Or that his biceps were bigger than my thighs. If I wasn't standing in a crowded penthouse next to Jesse and his smiling friend, he would've scared the shit out of me. "Nice to finally meet you." My voice practically squeaked. "Thank you for letting me use the penthouse tonight."

Talon must've picked up on my *oh shit* vibe because he chuckled. "Don't let Vikin' scare you. Unless you're afraid of proverbs, you've got nothin' to worry about."

Neil looked like a Viking but you wouldn't catch me pointing that out. "Proverbs?"

Without moving, Neil's gaze took in the paintings, passed Talon, then settled back on me. "'So vast is art, so narrow human wit.' And you are welcome." Deep and accented, his voice was almost haunting.

Talon grinned. "See? *Proverbs*." He drew the word out like he was talking dirty.

"Quote," Neil corrected. "Alexander Pope."

This guy read poems? He looked like he'd be more comfortable yielding a sledge hammer or gunning down enemies with a machine gun. "Well, thank you both for coming tonight. I really appreciate it."

Talon turned serious. "It's a great cause, darlin.'"

I glanced at Jesse but he was staring daggers across the room. I followed his line of sight and the douche from the hallway held up a drink at us. I tugged on Jesse's arm and spoke under my breath, "Ignore him."

Talon followed our gaze then laughed. "You've got to be shitting me." He glanced at Jesse. "Vegas?"

Douche's name was Vegas? How fitting.

Jesse wasn't amused. "Who is he?"

"2nd LAR Battalion," Talon rattled off the acronym as if they would know what he was talking about. "Vikin' knows him. I'm surprised you don't."

Neil tipped his chin at Vegas then glanced at Jesse. "La Mer Towers."

Jesse nodded as if he understood. "What's he doing here?"

"Probably workin.'" Talon smiled like he knew something we didn't. "I'm gonna give him shit. Be right back."

Now I was wondering who Vegas was and if I shouldn't have been rude to him. I didn't have time to ask because Franklin showed up in a panic.

"Hey man, my girl, she's like, *tipping*. Something's wrong, man. You gotta fix her. Like quick, before she falls off the wall."

"You don't have to bother Jesse, Franklin. I'll come look." I didn't even make it a step.

Jesse stopped me with a hand on my arm. "I've got it."

He nodded at Franklin. "Show me which painting." He followed a disheveled Franklin.

The second he was out of earshot, Neil spoke. "You will not get this charity off the ground without a facility."

He was so intimidating, I didn't even consider not answering him. "I'm going to rent kennel space."

"That does not give you a place to train the animals."

He was right. But it was all I could afford, so I was going to have to figure it out. "I'll make it work." But even with triple my minimum budget, it wouldn't cover leasing land to train the dogs. I was going to be at the mercy of dog parks and public areas. It wasn't ideal, but I was doing the best I could. The kennel would serve as my business address and legally, I was covered, so I was calling it a win.

"You have not thought this through."

Okay, now he was pissing me off. I'd done nothing *but* think this through. For two years, it'd been my life. "If you have a better idea, I'm all ears."

Talon came back and Neil didn't answer.

"You ready, Vikin'?"

Neil nodded.

Talon stepped up and kissed my cheek. "Later, darlin'. Good luck with the fundraiser. And tell Fixer he has competition." He tipped his chin toward the other side of the room and chuckled. "Looks like Vegas has his sights set on somethin' he wants."

I watched Talon and Neil leave. Then I made the mistake of glancing across the room. Taking a sip of his drink, Vegas, aka douche, winked at me over the rim of his glass.

"Hey." Jesse touched my arm. "Franklin's all set."

"One of his paintings was coming off the wall?" It wasn't

like Jesse to mess up something so simple as hanging a picture.

"No, someone must have bumped it. It just needed straightening." He glanced around. "Did Talon and Neil leave?"

"Yeah, they said to say good-bye." Sort of.

He exhaled then he focused on me and for the first time all night, it felt like my best friend was back. "So how's the show going? Did you meet your quota?"

The reality of the night kicked in and I grinned. "Triple."

His eyes went wide. "What?"

I could barely contain my excitement. I grabbed his lapels, went on tiptoe and leaned forward. "I made *triple* what I needed," I stage-whispered.

His lips landed on mine.

I gasped in shock and he didn't hesitate. Warm and soft, he tangled his tongue with mine as his rough, calloused hands cupped my face.

All I could think was *years.*

Years.

This was what I'd wanted from him. Exactly this. I'd wanted Jesse every way a woman could want a man. But this? *Now?* He was kissing me for the first time at my fundraiser? Confusion mingled with anger and about a hundred other different emotions as I stood there. My heart pounding, my hands at my sides, I just stood there.

He pulled back but his forehead touched mine. "*Olivia,*" he whispered.

I had no words.

Jesse frowned. "Shit." His hands tightened their hold on me. "*Shit.*"

I drew my lips between my teeth and my eyes welled.

"I'm sorry, Liv." He shook his head and dropped his hands. "I shouldn't have…." He trailed off and stepped back. "Triple. That's fantastic. I knew you could do it. I always believed in you. You know that." He took another step back. "I, um, I gotta go."

He turned and left.

And I let him.

FIVE

Alex

DAMN. I DIDN'T THINK THE BLOND BOB THE BUILDER had it in him. Ballsy move kissing the hot brunette in the middle of the fundraiser, but the walking out part? Fucking amateur.

"*Alex*," Trina cooed. "Where did you go?"

"Bathroom, babe. You can't come with me everywhere." I smiled to soften the blow, but not too much.

She dragged a finger over my chest. "Maybe I just want to come."

I decided to fuck with her. "That's extra."

She rubbed her tits against me for the hundredth time. "I'll pay double if we leave right now."

Twenty grand should've made my dick hard but it didn't. I was thinking about a feisty brunette in a tight dress and it was fucking with my game. Not to mention running into the medic from my unit in Afghanistan. I hadn't seen Talon since my last deployment, when he'd had to triage half my guys, and that wasn't shit I dwelled on. "Tell you what." I leaned toward Trina's ear and did something I never do. "Make it thirty and I'll fuck you all night."

She sucked in a breath and tried to smile past her Botox. "Yeesss," she purred.

31

"Alex?"

I glanced up and momentarily blanked before it hit me. Tuesday's four-grand cougar. "Hey." Damn, the brunette was throwing me off my game. I never forgot a face. I never forgot anything. "How's it going?"

Trina looked between us and scowled.

The cougar narrowed her eyes. "I thought you didn't take it out of the bedroom?"

Here we go. "Not sure what you're talking about, babe." Contingency plan A—smile like you fucking own it and deny everything.

Cougar's face twisted from mean bitch mach one to sinister in half a second flat. "I guess I didn't pay you enough." She looked at Trina. "Hope you get your money's worth. He's only good for two rounds."

Trina slapped Cougar.

The look of shock on her face was so fucking priceless, I burst out laughing. "*Damn.*" In retrospect, it wasn't the right reaction.

Trina turned on me.

Her arm swung out, I blocked the slap and suddenly, Olivia was at my side. "Mrs. Howards, Mrs. Pendleton!"

Cougar lunged at Trina.

I stepped back and an honest-to-God catfight broke out. Arms flying, hair pulling, heels kicking—I fucking grinned from ear to ear.

"*Ladies!*" Olivia went dead white. "Please don't do this at my fundraiser!" She glanced accusingly at me. "Did you start this? Are they fighting over you?"

Her fundraiser? I polished off my drink and set my glass on the bar. "Not my fault." Not technically. And what the hell did she mean by her fundraiser?

Cougar kicked Trina.

"Oh my God." Olivia sidestepped them and grabbed my arm. *"Do something."*

Trina got a solid left hook to Cougar's eye.

I didn't even care. Screw my client. The brunette had her hand on me and I was fucking running with it. I flexed my bicep and smiled at her. "I'm not getting paid to break them up."

Her lips formed a sexy little O. *"What?"*

I wanted those lips, preferably wrapped around my cock. "What's it worth to you?"

A dress ripped and Olivia flinched. "You want me to *pay you?"*

"Go out with me." I had no fucking shame.

"I'm not going out with you!" She tried to shove me toward the women. "Stop this! *She's your date."*

Exhaling, I shook my head. Ten, twenty, shit—thirty grand—it wasn't even a choice. I let it go. "No, she's not." Was I out of my fucking mind? "Have dinner with me and I'll break them up."

"Fine! I'll pay you. *Just make it stop."*

Not ideal, but this could work. "Five," I named my price.

"Five hundred?" She practically levitated then recoiled when Cougar kicked Trina and she fell back into the wall near a shit painting.

I smiled. "No, grand."

Cougar rushed Trina and the painting hit the floor.

"Ohmigod!" Olivia squealed. *"Stop them."*

I didn't move. "Five grand?"

The two women dropped to a wrestle hold and rolled on the floor.

Olivia lunged for the fallen painting and grabbed it before the women rolled on top of it. "Yes! Ohmigod, *yes*."

I glanced at the cougar war on the ground and shook my head because I was a fucking idiot. I was going to lose two more clients this week but I didn't give a single fuck. I had a hook in the brunette and I was already scheming.

I reached down and plucked up Trina. "Great job, babe. You showed her who's boss. Proud of you." She stiffened but then the fight left her. "Come on, show's over." I took a few strides to the elevator and hit the button with my elbow. "I think you've had enough fun for one night." The doors slid open and I stepped in and set her on her feet. "Your driver will take you home. We'll call tonight a wash. No charge." I winked and hit the lobby button then stepped back out of the elevator.

"Alex, *wait*—" Trina reached out.

The doors slid shut and I pivoted.

Everyone was staring.

I fake smiled. "Show's over, folks. Drink up and buy some paintings. Let's give those vets what they deserve!"

Silence.

My gaze landed on Olivia's devastated face.

Fuck.

"Don't leave me hanging, people." Then I did something I hadn't done since I'd walked away from the Marines. "*Semper Fi.*" I saluted.

A few *Oorahs* echoed through the crowd and everyone slowly went back to whatever the fuck they were doing.

Everyone except Olivia.

She stood in the middle of that room looking like she was about to burst into tears and damn it, even though I didn't throw a punch, I felt responsible for the catfight.

I pushed through the crowd and put my arm around her shoulders. "Smile, babe. Five grand says I'm your daddy tonight."

She looked up at me and maybe, just maybe, my approach was off.

"It's ruined," she seethed. "*You ruined it.*"

"All right, you don't have to call me daddy. That's extra anyway." I steered her toward the bar and signaled the bartender. "Whiskey for the lady, neat. Make it a double." I ignored the bartender's disapproving look. "It's not ruined, I promise." I glanced around to make sure. "Everyone's moved on. Let's have a drink."

Her half growl with the unshed tears in her eyes was worse than if she'd busted out sobbing. "I'm not drinking tonight."

"Trust me, one drink won't—"

Her back stiffened, her nostrils flared and she let loose. "*Trust you?*" She shoved my arm off her shoulders. "You arrogant, piece of shit *asshole*. Those women were fighting over you!" she whisper-hissed.

Shit. "Okay, first, they were fighting because one slapped the other." She didn't need to know they were both my clients. "Second, I'll admit to the arrogance, maybe even the asshole part. But *piece of shit's* a little extreme, don't you think? I wasn't the one pulling hair or bitch slapping."

"You just stood there!"

Goddamn she was hot when she was pissed. The corner of my mouth tipped up. "You have to admit, it was entertaining."

Her face twisted. "No, it *wasn't.*"

Four-grand cougar walked up.

Christ, I'd forgotten about her.

Her hair straightened, her dress put back together, the

murderous look on her face was the only giveaway that she was about to unleash. "You lying bastard," she practically spat at me.

Contingency plan B—distract. I smiled, put my arm around Olivia and used the first bullshit distraction that popped into my head. "Have you met my girlfriend, Olivia?"

Cougar went beet red.

Olivia stiffened. "Mrs. Pendleton, I'm sorry about what happ—"

Oh fuck no. She wasn't going to apologize to Cougar. "You don't have any reason to be sorry, Olivia. You weren't the one throwing kicks and pulling hair." I squeezed Olivia's shoulder and gave Cougar a warning look.

Cougar's glare swung to Olivia. "You stupid girl," she spat out. "Do you know—"

I didn't let her finish that sentence. No fucking way did she get to throw insults after she'd rolled around on the floor. Not to mention, I knew exactly where she was going with it. She'd tell Olivia who and what I was quicker than I could make a woman moan. I wasn't ashamed of what I did, but for the first time in three years, I wished I was some asshole banker in a bad suit. "We're done here." I grabbed the whiskey the bartender set down.

Olivia's hands went up in supplication. "Mrs. Pendleton, I'm so sorry about the incident. Please, let me make it up to you. I'll replace your dress or whatever I can do. You know I'm good for it. I've worked for you for years, you know I'll take care of it."

She worked for Cougar?

Cougar fumed. "This charity will never—"

I whisked Olivia toward the farthest wall from the bar and stopped in front of a shitty painting.

"You told my boss I was dating you," she growled. "After she *fought* over you."

"She wasn't fighting over me." I tipped the glass of whiskey to her lips. "Drink."

She didn't have a choice if she didn't want to make another scene. She took a sip but then pulled back and coughed, her face twisting as the alcohol slid down her throat. "That's shit whiskey."

I fought a smile and gestured at the painting in front of us. "How about this landscape?"

"You can drop the act. I know you're not buying anything." She shoved my arm off and half turned but then swore under breath. "*Shit.* Now she's talking to two of my buyers."

I glanced over my shoulder and Cougar wasn't just talking, she was glaring and pointing at Olivia.

Opportunity was a beautiful thing.

"Make this look good, sweetness." I leaned down before Olivia could protest and dragged my lips across her ear as I whispered, "Smile. Show everyone you don't give a fuck about her or the catfight." I kissed her cheek, lingering longer than I should because she didn't just smell good, her scent was intoxicating as hell. Not like overpriced perfume but like purity... and challenge.

She bared her teeth. "You lied to her."

"Is that supposed to be a smile?" I chuckled. "Come on, you can do better than that." I pulled her closer. "Where's the sweet innocence you had for Bob the Builder?"

Her eyes tight, her sneer upped a notch. "His name is Jesse and I'm not done talking about that stunt you just pulled with my boss."

I turned the tables on her. "You sure you should be

working for someone like that?" I glanced over my shoulder for effect then made a face. "She seems a little unhinged."

"She's not unhinged. She's rich." Her hands went to her hips and she said *rich* like it was a crime.

My gaze lingered on the lush curves her hands were getting to touch and I licked my lips. "So having money makes it okay to get down and dirty at a fundraiser?" Arguing with her was the most fun I'd had in months.

"No, but—"

I leaned toward her and lowered my voice. "No buts, beautiful." Damn, she smelled incredible. "And no excuses. We all gotta play by the rules sometime." I lingered a second longer to see if she'd pull away.

She didn't.

I straightened, putting just enough distance between us so she'd notice. "So which painting do you like?" Women always wanted what they thought they couldn't have.

She suspiciously eyed the half a foot I put between us then glanced at the painting. When she spoke, her voice was calmer but still had an edge. "I don't have a favorite."

Slow, calculated, half my mouth tipped up. "That's too bad." I waited until she looked at me. "I was hoping you'd tell me what turned you on."

For half a second, she didn't react. Then she crossed her arms, her tits pushed together and the million fantasies I was envisioning kicked into high gear.

Her clear blue eyes gazed up at me "Do you ever stop flirting?"

I dropped my half smile. "Not with you."

She stared at me. No words, no pretense, she simply stared.

My heart rate kicked up and I fought to keep from taking her into my arms. All I wanted to do was touch her, anywhere she'd let me. "Want to know my favorite part of the evening so far?"

She ignored my question. "You do know you're wasting your time, right?"

I moved a few inches closer. "You're not a waste of time, gorgeous."

"How would you know?" She didn't move back. "You don't even know me." Her head dropped slightly.

She wasn't protesting. She wasn't pushing me away. She was curious and I saw my in. I handed the drink to a passing waiter and lowered my voice. "Right now."

"Excuse me?"

"This." I dragged my gaze across her lips then stared into her deep blue eyes. "This is my favorite part of the evening." I was so close, I could feel her breath on me.

"I would've thought the catfight…." Her words died on her lips as she looked up and met my gaze.

I went for broke. "I kiss better than your boyfriend."

Her expression didn't change but she sucked in a quick breath. "He's not my boyfriend and I'm not…."

Thank fuck. "Interested?" I slid a hand down her arm, barely touching her. Just like I knew it would, gooseflesh broke out across her soft skin. "You sure about that? Because I know how to kiss." And fuck. "And lover boy? He didn't do a damn thing right because he had no game." I grasped her hand and put it around my neck as I walked her three steps back and around a corner for privacy.

"Wh-what are you doing?" She glanced around nervously.

"Showing you how I would've held you." I cupped her face. "Told you how beautiful you are." I held her gaze for a heartbeat. "Stunning actually." I trailed my fingers down her back. "I would've pulled you in close and let you know I wanted more." I grasped her hip and brought her flush against my semi. "Then I would've kissed you...," I paused for effect before dropping the hook, "like I meant it."

My hand tightened its grip on her face, my fingers dug into her ass and I kissed her, Alex Vega style.

I thrust my tongue into her shocked mouth and gave her something she'd never had. Something that netted me a seven-figure bank account and a lifestyle I wouldn't trade for anything. I gave her the experience and control women paid thousands for. I gave her me.

Then shit went sideways.

Whiskey, purity and sweet fucking innocence reared up and punched me in the gut. Air left my lungs, my brain misfired and I surged like a tidal wave. Same as that fucking Bob the Builder tool, I grasped her face with both hands. But the similarity stopped there. I wasn't timid. I dominated her sweet mouth and demanded her tongue in return. I swept through her heat and groaned out of sheer fucking need. My dick throbbed and I kissed her harder.

Small hands curled into the collar of my shirt as she went on tiptoe and kissed me back.

She kissed me back.

I ground my hips like I'd won the damn lottery and she moaned into my mouth. Every ounce of fire she dished out in attitude morphed into sex vixen and client or not, I wanted to fuck her right then and there.

I bit her bottom lip and spoke against her mouth. "That's it, sweetness. Show me how good I make you feel."

"You're not," she panted, "a good kisser." Her hands landed on my chest and she pushed me away.

SIX

Olivia

MY LEGS TREMBLED, MY THONG WAS SOAKED AND MY nipples were hard. I sucked in a breath. Then another. He wasn't a good kisser, he was an amazing kisser. But I hated guys like him.

That fucking kiss though.

Jesse didn't kiss like that. He didn't even come close to kissing like that. And I didn't care what Douche said, my boss was fighting over him. And holy fucking shit, the equipment he was packing below the belt? If that was half as large as I thought it was, *oh my God*. But still. What the hell was I doing letting him kiss me like that?

He grasped my chin like he had a right to and swept his thumb over my bottom lip. "You're sexy when you lie."

His stupid words kicked some sense back into me. "Do those bullshit lines work on your cougar girlfriends? I would've thought with age comes wisdom. But what do I know? I'm only twenty-four, unlike your last conquest." What a player. I couldn't believe I'd kissed him back. I pulled away and stepped into the main space.

I felt his body heat a second before his breath touched my ear. "Jealous?"

41

Intending to tell him to fuck off, I spun. But when he laid his sexy-as-hell smile on me and I caught sight of those eyes, eyes I could get lost in for days, the edge to my voice disappeared. "Of what? A disease?" From across the room, my boss glanced at me but she didn't sneer. In fact, she looked smug. *Really* smug.

Mr. Perfect Kisser gently cupped the side of my face like I meant something to him. "It's not the dark ages, sweetness. A little fun doesn't mean you're going to catch something."

Oh, there was a whole lot I could catch from him, none of it good. I swatted his hand away. "You bidding on anything or were you just here to be some rich old lady's arm candy?"

"Are you admitting I'm arm candy?" His eyes glinted with mischief.

He was a lot more than arm candy, I was sure. I knew my boss had a penchant for young guys. There'd been a string of them in the two years I'd been walking her dogs and volunteering at the kennel she owned through her countless real estate holdings. She couldn't even be bothered to hide her infidelity from her husband—not that his mental acuity was as sharp as it was before the dementia set in, but still. I hated my boss. She had no respect for anyone, not even her dogs that she treated like accessories, but I needed to be in her good graces. She was the only one who was willing to rent me kennel space to get my charity going.

I shook my head. "Just leave."

He leaned closer and his scent, clean and dangerous, surrounded me. "Pay me and I will."

"Are you serious?" Shit. "I'm not paying you. You're lucky I don't call the cops on you."

"For what?" He grinned like he knew he had me, because he did.

"Sexual assault, being an asshole, drinking and driving— pick one. I don't care how good you look in your expensive suit, you're not getting five grand out of me. This is a fund-raiser, not a free-for-all." The more I thought about it, the an-grier I got. He'd totally used the catfight to his advantage. "In fact, why don't you do something for someone else for once and buy a damn painting that supports the needs of veter-ans who actually served our country?" I glanced at his ridic-ulously well-defined chest that was stretching his perfectly pressed shirt in all the right places. "Looks like you can afford it." I was over him and his sexy fucking smile.

"Not going to work. I already paid my dues." He saluted me. "Eight years, sweetness."

I'd heard his *Semper Fi*, everyone had heard it, but I'd thought he was bullshitting. He was cocky and arrogant and shit… his shoulders were parade stance straight. Damn it. I should've seen it. "Marines." I didn't have to ask. He was just like my brother used to be… before his last deployment.

"And here I thought you'd be impressed." He held his hand over his heart as if he were wounded.

I scowled. The bids were shutting down and I needed to go. "I don't have time to waste on you." I spun and he caught my arm.

"What exactly is the charity for?"

"Canine Watch."

He raised a sexy eyebrow and waited.

I sighed. "Canine Watch is a charity that will train and provide PTSD service dogs to veterans at no cost." I'd said the name and explanation so many times over the past year,

I'd lost count, but it never stopped being hurtful every time the words left my mouth, knowing my brother was gone.

Mr. Perfect Kisser had the decency to look impressed. "No kidding?"

I took in his flawlessly put together appearance. His clothes, his watch, his gym abs—he dripped money and composure. Not even my hands on him had left a hair out of place, but me? I probably looked like I'd walked through a swamp. And my stupid body kept tingling like it needed more of what this player was selling. "I don't joke about my charity."

"So it is your charity."

"That's what I said. Now if you'll let go of my arm, I need to wrap up the bids." And make sure every piece sold. And get away from him.

He tipped his chin at the painting he thought was a landscape. "How much for this one?"

"Thirty-five thousand." At least, that was the bid last time I checked.

He turned to face the painting without letting go of me. "You think it's worth that?"

"That's not what it's worth. That's the highest bid. If you want it, you need to bid thirty-six thousand."

He seemed to ponder this a moment. "Tell you what. You go out with me and I'll forget about the five grand you owe me and I'll bid forty for the painting."

"I already told you I don't owe you anything and I'm not going out with you." Was he seriously going to pay forty grand just to get me to go out with him?

He let loose with his million-dollar smile. "It's the opportunity of a lifetime, sweetness."

Unbelievable. "You're a piece of work, you know that?" His hand coasted down his shirt and over his hard abs.

"So I've been told."

I pulled my arm free and walked away before I did anything stupid, like agree to go out with him. I made it exactly three paces when Franklin stopped me.

"Dude." Panic leaked out of his pores. "You've *got* to anchor it. It's like, falling." His head started pendulum-ing. "I can't...." His hands went through his hair. "I can't sell it like that. I can't sell *any* of them. No, no, no, dude. I can't hang." He reached for the toilet water piece as if he were going to grab it and run.

"Franklin," I warned. "You take that down and you're not going to have *anything* happy to put in your pocket." I glanced at his pants pocket. "You get me?"

His shoulders slumped and he hung his head. "Duuuude."

"I'm not a dude, Franklin. We went over this." I didn't care who was watching. That painting had sold for the highest bid and I wasn't letting him walk out with it.

He sighed and glanced at me but his eyes weren't focused. "I need my happy. I can't paint without my happy." He dropped his gaze to his shoes. "But Cecile? She's *un*happy."

Mr. Perfect Kisser stepped up beside me and I swore he was holding back a grin. "Who's Cecile?"

Franklin nodded at the painting and sighed.

I pointed at the toilet water piece. "The title is *Down Under*."

Franklin looked at me like I was the one who was crazy. "*Well, yeah.* Who do you think I went down on?"

Mr. Perfect Kisser choked back laughter. "You went down on a woman and painted a brown painting about it?"

Franklin swung his gaze toward him as if noticing him for the first time. "Have you seen Cecile? She's like…" He mouthed *whoa* and made a waving motion with his hands. "Dirty," he whispered.

Oh my God.

Mr. Perfect Kisser grinned. "Dirty talker, huh? She hot?"

Franklin started nodding again. "Ohhh man, like every other word out of her mouth is *shit*. But she doesn't say shit, she's all, '*shiiiiiit.*'" He threw his head back and moaned the word out like he was coming. A silence fell over the room, and he abruptly picked his head up and slapped his hands together dramatically. "And then she hits you."

"Dude." Mr. Perfect Kisser shook his head in disapproval.

"I know, right? It's hard core, man. I'm like, I'm all beat up and shit." Franklin glanced at me. "I need my happy. And Cecile? She's not happy."

Mr. Perfect Kisser tipped his chin at the two cases of water that sat under the painting that I'd hauled up and thrown a table cloth over. "What's with that?"

Franklin looked accusingly at me. "I told you it should be sandbags."

Mr. Perfect Kisser coughed over a laugh. "Sandbags?"

"Shut up," I hissed. "Franklin, that's your anchor. That's the code inspector's *approved* anchor." I made every word up.

He scratched his head. "It's like, official?"

I bit my tongue. "It doesn't get any more official."

Franklin inhaled deeply. "Cecile hurts me."

Mr. Perfect Kisser slapped him on the back. "You need a new girlfriend, man."

Franklin looked up at him like a little kid. "You think?"

"I know."

"She makes my dick sore," Franklin confessed.

"All the good ones do." Mr. Perfect Kisser didn't miss a beat as he commiserated with Franklin's bizarre comment like it was normal as hell and as if a room full of people weren't staring. "They don't call it *fucking* for nothing." He ushered Franklin toward the bar. "Come on, you need a drink." He glanced over his shoulder at me and winked. "You coming, sweetness?"

"Yeah," I lied. "Be right there."

"Olivia?"

I turned and the caterer I'd hired politely kept her eyes off the spectacle that was Franklin and Mr. Perfect Kisser. "I'm almost wrapped up. Do you need anything else? The bar is freshly stocked. You should be fine even if the guests stay late."

"Thanks, Mandy. Let me grab your check."

"Sure, take your time. I have a few things to wrap up. I'll be in the staging area."

She smiled almost nervously and I veered off toward the back of the apartment. My head spinning, I rushed to one of the back rooms Jesse had put a lock on for me. I slipped my key from my bra and used it to get inside.

I didn't want to think about Jesse right now. And I especially didn't want to think about his kiss in comparison to… *shit.* I didn't even know Mr. Perfect Kisser's name. It was official. I was a slut.

I grabbed the check, locked the door behind me and found the caterer to pay her. As I made my way back, laughter, rich and deep, rang out across the space and my skin tingled.

"No way, dude!" Franklin's face creased with a wide smile, his eyes actually focused, and he looked almost normal as he stood next to Mr. Perfect Kisser in a circle of five women.

"Would I lie about something like that?" Mr. Perfect Kisser tipped his drink toward Franklin.

"Totally not, dude." He nodded enthusiastically. "No way."

A tall blonde pressed up against Mr. Perfect Kisser's arm. "Tell us another story." Her pouty lips were inches from his neck.

Mrs. Pendleton snapped her fingers at the blonde. "Let's go."

The blonde rolled her eyes but she and the rest of the girls trailed after my boss like ducklings.

Anxiety prickled up my spine and I glanced around. I'd been so focused on Mr. Perfect Kisser and the girl pressing up on him that I hadn't immediately realized the crowd had diminished, like seriously diminished.

Mrs. Pendleton waltzed past me and sneered. "In case you didn't already figure it out, *you're fired.*"

The elevator doors shut on her and her entourage.

Cold dread hit my stomach as I scrambled for my phone. My hands shaking, I opened the app.

Every single bid was gone.

SEVEN

Alex

THE ARTIST THAT SMELLED LIKE WEED AND TWO-DAY-old sex exhaled. "Dude. The charity chick doesn't look so good."

I stared at Olivia as she went stock-still. Cougar and her entourage waltzed to the elevator and with one last bitch face directed at Olivia, the doors closed.

Olivia whipped her phone out of her bra and her fingers flew across the screen. Then her arms dropped to her sides and her phone slipped from her hands.

"Duuuude." The freak artist set his drink on the bar. "I know that face. Shit's about to get *heavy*."

Olivia was on the move before the last word left his mouth. Her phone forgotten on the floor, she strode to the shit painting with the crates of water under it and plucked it off the wall.

She was opening the balcony slider before the artist moved.

"Whoa, dude, whoa!"

Olivia hurled the painting over the railing.

"*Cecile!*"

Without breaking stride, Olivia was behind the bar

shoving the bartender out of the way. "You can go, you're not getting paid overtime." She hefted the bottle of whiskey and spared the dumbstruck idiot one glance. "*Now.*"

He grabbed his tips and both he and the artist made a break for the elevator, except the bartender wasn't muttering to himself as he pulled at his hair. The last few remaining people followed them and a second later, the packed elevator left and we were alone.

I leaned on the bar as Olivia threw back straight from the bottle. "You want to talk about it?"

She ignored me and took another huge swig.

"I'm all for getting your buzz on, sweetness, but I'm not a fan of babysitting. You got a plan for all that alcohol?"

She sucked air in through her teeth. "Fuck you."

"Just say when." I smiled but she didn't notice.

She drank again.

I should've left her to it, but that fucking kiss was imprinted on my brain and my dick wanted to find out what all the hype was about. "You threw my favorite painting out."

No reaction.

"I kinda liked the dirty little Cecile, even if she was a sadist."

Olivia stared at me as she lifted the bottle to her lips and took a massive swig.

A hammered chick wasn't a fun chick. "Not gonna lie." I snatched the bottle from her grasp. "I don't buy into the whole fem domme, male sub role play."

If looks could kill, her gaze slayed me twice then spit fire on the carnage.

I shrugged. "But hey, if it'll get you to talk to me, I'm game," I lied. I didn't do that shit. Ever.

"Give. Me. That *bottle*."

Christ she was sexy when she was pissed. "Not what I was aiming for when I wanted you to talk." Taking the bottle with me, I went to retrieve her phone, but I'd neglected to lock down the other twenty bottles at the bar. When I turned back toward her, she had the vodka.

She pulled the stopper out and threw it across the bar before taking a long swill. The coughing fit that followed spurred me into action.

"Hey, hey, hey, arms up." I grabbed the bottle and set it down then encircled her wrists and raised her arms above her head. "Breathe, baby, in through your nose."

She tried to wrench free. "I'm not—" She coughed. "—*your baby*."

Jesus, she was small. "We can remedy that later, but right now, take a breath."

She coughed once more. "You. *You ruined it*."

Arms above her head, her dark hair falling out of its twist, blue eyes bright with tears, she was stunning—totally fucking stunning. And pissed as hell at me for some reason. "Check it, sweetness. I didn't throw the profits off the balcony."

She wrenched free and picked up the vodka.

Momentarily taken off guard, her swing didn't register until it was too late to do anything except duck. The bottle flew past my head and slammed into the wall behind me. Shattering glass exploded through the silence and echoed like a motherfucker. "Hey!" I snapped.

Another bottle flew in my direction.

Fuck this.

I grabbed her as she reached for a third bottle. My arms

went around her from behind, and I lifted her off her feet, easily overpowering her. "Calm down," I demanded.

"No!" She kicked me in the shin.

Fuck.

My arm hit the back of her knees and I brought her legs up as I picked her up. In one swift movement, I tossed her ass on the bar, stepped between her legs and grabbed her wrists. "Kick me again," I warned, "and you'll regret it."

"Let me go!" She arched her back violently then tried to head butt me.

I pushed her down on the bar, covered her chest with mine and got in her face. "Calm down."

"You fucking *asshole!*"

I kissed her.

She gasped and my tongue sank into her angry, hot mouth.

I stroked through her fire once, twice….

Her tongue stroked me back.

I released her wrists and small hands gripped my hair with the force of a tornado. Strong legs wrapped around my hips, her thighs anchored to my waist, and she threw herself into the kiss. Teeth gnashing, hips thrusting, back arching, a hurricane couldn't touch her.

I fucking growled as I grasped the back of her knee and shoved her leg wide. Rotating my hips, I dry humped the shit out of her as I ground my dick between her legs. Grasping her jaw, I spoke against her mouth. "Tell me to fuck you."

Her arms tightened around my neck and she bit at my bottom lip. "*Fuck me,*" she panted.

I shoved my tongue into her mouth as I yanked her dress up. I broke the kiss only long enough to pull the material over her head and drag her red thong down her sexy legs. Taking in the sight of her bare pussy, already glistening with desire, I thought I was in fucking heaven until I saw her tits. Lush and so goddamn real, I groaned.

"Sweet Jesus." I pulled her bra down just enough to expose what I wanted then I drew her hard nipple between my teeth.

"*Ahhh.*" Her back arched and her eyes fluttered shut.

I'd fucked a lot of women, but in that moment, not a single one of them stood out. I didn't get attached, ever. But this woman? All fire and attitude, with a sexy red lace bra over that perfect fucking rack? *Goddamn.* She was already burned into my memory as if she'd branded me. "You're fucking gorgeous, sweetness." I'd been calling her sweetness to make fun of her attitude but the joke was on me. There was nothing about her sexy little body that wasn't sweet as sin.

She struggled with my belt. "Pants… off."

I grabbed a condom out of my pocket. I didn't think about her not being a client or about the fact that she'd be the first woman I'd fucked in three years who hadn't paid me. I didn't think about shit except getting inside of her.

In a move so practiced, I could write a book about it, I unzipped my pants and pulled my cock out. Stroking myself with one hand, I put the corner of the foil between my teeth and ripped open the Magnum. Sheathed in seconds, I grabbed the backs of her knees and brought her thighs around my waist. Then I did what I'd wanted to do since I first saw her. I undid the clip in her hair. Waves of rich brown fell over her pale shoulders and the scent of jasmine and woman hit me square in the chest. Inhaling, I reached between her legs.

Jesus.

My fingers sank into tight, wet heat and I groaned. Stroking through her folds, I rubbed my thumb over her clit and she jerked against my touch.

She was so fucking hot, lies and bullshit compliments didn't roll off my tongue. I wasn't calculating every move for effect. I didn't choreograph every touch. I didn't drag her to the brink only to pull back and ask for more money. I wasn't even thinking about someone hotter so I could stay hard.

I was gripping the shaft of my cock and dragging the head through her desire, wondering how fucking tight she would feel around me. "You ready for me, sweetness?"

She spread her legs wider. "Stop *talking*."

I thrust deep.

Her back bowed, her mouth opened on a silent gasp and she gripped two handfuls of my tailored suit as my cock sank into the tightest pussy I'd ever been in. The sultry haze in her eyes disappeared in a nanosecond and tears welled.

Shit.

I grasped the side of her face and stilled, forcing myself not to pull back and thrust even deeper. "Shh, baby, it's okay." Something that was too damn close to emotion settled in my chest and fuck if I didn't want to hurt her. "Give it a minute. You'll adjust."

Her muscles clenched around me as her sexy, breathless voice filtered into my head. "What's your name?"

The side of my mouth tipped up. "Alex."

Her hips eased back but her heels dug into my ass. Then she suddenly yanked on my jacket and used the leverage of her grip to pull herself upright against me. My dick slammed all the way home as her lips touched my ear. "I hate you, *Alex*."

I froze. For half a second.

Then my nostrils flared and I gripped a handful of her hair. Hard. "You think I'm going to let you come now?"

"Fuck you," she hissed, grinding against me.

I pulled and her head fell back. My teeth dragged up her throat but my dick was still as fuck. I didn't know what the fuck had just happened, and I didn't care. She wanted to play games? "Oh," I warned, "I'm gonna fuck you." I bit her ear. "And I'm going to do it hard and fast." She was about to see exactly how fucked this could get.

Her pussy already pulsing on me, she moaned.

"I'm going to show you every inch of what I can do for you." I pulled out slow and kissed her neck like I wasn't pissed as hell. She tried to drag me back but I was in control now. My hand on her chest, my teeth grazing her hard nipple but not giving her enough pressure to make it worth it, I held her back.

"You can't do shit for me."

I forced a chuckle, pulled her off the bar and spun her. "You can't begin to imagine what I can do to you." I kicked her legs apart then I stepped back. Goddamn, her ass was fucking perfect. "Put your hands on the bar." Calculated, controlled, I lowered my voice. "Or walk out."

She didn't hesitate. Her hands gripped the edge and she pushed her ass out. "You fucking walk out."

"I will." I grabbed her waist with one hand and shoved two fingers inside her with the other. "After I fuck you."

"Good." She tried and failed to fight a moan.

I worked her exactly where I knew she needed it and leaned down to her ear. "You hate this?" Her desire dripped down my hand.

"Yes," she breathed.

"I'm just getting started." I abruptly pulled my hand out, fisted my cock, then thrust all the way home. My head fell back, the air left my lungs and for one fucking heartbeat, I lost my mind. Her tight little cunt clamped down and all I could think was it'd be a goddamn dream to feel her come all over me.

But she hated me.

No one hated me.

Women fucking loved me. They paid thousands to get what this little bitch was getting for free.

Impaled, her body hanging on my junk, she was humping my shit before I even got a chance to work her into a frenzy. I told myself she was no different than the scores of women I'd already fucked, but deep down I knew that was bullshit.

I wound my fingers through the soft waves of her hair and wrapped it around my hand. Dragging my mouth up her spine and over her shoulder, I worked my hips. Slow and measured, I ground deep and used my teeth right where her neck met her collarbone. Ignoring the complete and total mind fuck this woman was giving me, I whispered in her ear, "I'm going to ride the fuck out of you."

But I wasn't going to let her come. No fucking way.

I thrust hard, once, twice, then I did what I never do. I fucked for me. I held her down and pounded into her with everything I had. She was so goddamn tight and wet, her pussy didn't fit my cock like a glove, it fucking owned it.

My balls drew tight, my muscles tensed and the first pulse of my orgasm shot into the condom.

Then her pussy clenched around me, hard.

Goddamn.

The second pulse hit me and I blindly drew my hand

back. The sound of my palm connecting with her ass finished me off. I barely pulled out before she went all the way off.

"What?" She frantically reached behind her. "*No.*"

I whipped the condom off and tied it. It was in my pocket and my pants were zipped in two seconds flat.

"You fucking *asshole.*" She glared over her shoulder at me. "I'm not done!"

I gave her the smile that said I didn't give a fuck. "I am."

With one hand holding the edge of the bar for support, she reached for the nearest bottle, lifted it to her lips and downed three gulps.

Marginally less pissed after blowing my load, I took in the sight for what it was. A hot-as-fuck chick in heels and a red lace bra getting shitty.

I palmed my keys. "You're not driving. Get dressed. I'll take you home."

She turned toward me and stumbled. "You're right, I'm not driving." She set the bottle on the bar, grabbed her dress off the floor and yanked it over her head. Then she leaned forward and narrowed her gorgeous eyes at me. "Because I don't have a car anymore. I sold it to pay for this party." Squaring her shoulders, she gave me the finger then spun and teetered to the elevator. Jabbing at the call button, she threw one last insult over her shoulder. "And I don't want a ride home from an asshole who sucks in bed."

"We weren't in a bed, *sweetness.*" I bit the pet name out even though I knew showing emotion was a fucking amateur move.

"Thank God." The elevator doors opened, she stepped inside and a second later she was gone.

Jesus fuck, I was losing my touch.

I ran a hand through my hair and noticed her phone on the bar. I picked it up and the screen didn't even have a lock code. One swipe and I saw the app. All the paintings in the show were listed with a minimum opening bid and a buy now price.

Not a single painting had sold.

I glanced around the makeshift gallery as understanding hit me right in the gut. "God-fucking-dammit."

I bought every painting.

EIGHT

Olivia

REVENGE FUCK.
That's all that was.
Revenge.
Or hate fuck. Fucking both. Because fuck my boss and her fucking cougar-ette boyfriend and her stupid fucking cat-fight and *firing me*, and fuck the kennel and, *ohmigod*, fuck these stupid, *stupid* fucking heels.

I kicked them off.

I wanted to leave them on the damn sidewalk but some-where in my alcohol-infused brain I reasoned I could sell them on consignment. *Consignment.* Dead broke and drunk, doing the walk of shame with no underwear because I fucked the hottest guy I'd ever laid eyes on, and I was thinking about how much I could get for my shoes.

Fuck my life.

And fuck Alex. I hated him. *Hated him.* And I'd let him fuck me? *I'd begged him for it?* Because my life hadn't just shit the bed enough, I needed to sabotage every last thing to make sure I was good and fucked? What the hell was wrong with me? Was that how I handled a kiss from Jesse? By throwing away my entire future and fucking another guy? *Oh my God.*

59

I couldn't even think straight.

And the stupid pavement was still warm under my feet at ten o'clock at night. I'd better enjoy it because in a few weeks when rent was due, I'd be moving north to live with my mother. Maybe I should just ask Jesse if I could go to Ocala then fuck him too.

I snorted.

Jesse. Who had a girlfriend but kissed me but was supposed to be my best friend, *Jesse*.

I yanked open the door to the old art deco apartment building I lived in then slammed it shut behind me. I hated the seafoam green walls but the thought of leaving them to live somewhere colder made me want to cry. And the fact that I was more upset about that than not selling a single stupid painting should have registered as a red flag, but it didn't. I wasn't even pissed anymore about the charity going up in flames before it got off the ground. I was pissed about my apartment.

I stomped up the stairs and made it all the way to my door when I realized I didn't have my keys… or my phone. "*Shit.*"

My front door opened.

"Olivia."

Jesse. Big, strong, tall, blond Jesse. He had a key. He'd always had a key. But I didn't have a key to his place. I never had. And that didn't seem weird until this very second.

I looked up at brown eyes that used to be my anchor. "Why are you inside my apartment?"

His gaze briefly scanned the length of my body then his eyebrows drew together. "You wanted me to wait in the hall?"

Hall. Street. At his place. "You could've called."

"You weren't answering your phone."

I patted myself down. "Because I don't have it."

"You lost it?" His expression said it all.

I had never lost anything. Not even my wits. But apparently tonight was a whole new ball game, complete with suckass decisions. And my traitorous pussy clenched just thinking about them. "Lost, left, what difference does it make?" I was a failure. At *everything*.

"Are you drunk?"

He said *drunk* like it was a four-letter word. And to him, maybe it was. I'd never gotten drunk with Jesse. In fact, he rarely drank anything besides water. "Who only drinks water anyway?"

He sighed and pulled his lips into his mouth. I used to like when he did that. It looked cute. Or something. But now it didn't look cute. It didn't look like anything except a big ole comparison to a dark-haired, giant-dicked stranger. A stranger who'd ruined everything I'd worked my ass off for the past year. Every second of my life had been consumed with getting this charity off the ground just to prove I wasn't a horrible person. But I was. Horrible. I fucked strangers and I let my brother die. And I needed more alcohol. Or sex. Or a new life.

"Come on." Jesse gently took my arm and pulled me inside my own apartment. "Let's get you some water."

Water. "It doesn't fix everything, you know that, right?"

He shut the door and locked it then looked down at me. "What's going on, Olivia?"

"Uh-oh," I mocked him. "Now you're serious." I lowered my voice to mimic him. "What's going on, Olivia? Drink some water, Olivia. Answer your phone, Olivia." I wrenched my arm out of his grasp. "Go kiss your fucking girlfriend. I'm sure she likes it." I wanted my couch. And some Chinese food. And more alcohol.

"Is that what this is about?" he accused. "You're angry because I kissed you?"

I threw my shoes down and spun. "I'm angry because you should've kissed me *years* ago, but you didn't. And now we're here, and here?" I swept my arm around my small apartment. "*Sucks.*"

He took two giant strides and pulled me into his arms.

I burst into tears.

"Shh, it's okay, Liv. I'm sorry. We'll go back to how things were."

I cried harder.

He was holding me. My Jesse. After I'd let that asshole fuck me and my future. Nothing was going to be okay. Everything was ruined. *Everything.* "I let my brother down," I sobbed.

Strong, familiar hands swept my hair from my face and warm lips touched my forehead. "No you didn't. He let you down."

I froze. "What did you say?"

Jesse sighed. "He let you down, Liv. He let everyone who loved him down."

"No." I pulled back. "You don't get to say that about him. How can you even think that?" He'd never said anything bad about my brother, ever.

Jesse grasped my shoulders. "He made a choice, Liv. But he didn't have to make that choice. He could've reached out. He could've come to me or you or your mom, but he didn't. What he did was selfish."

I shoved him away. "How dare you!" He didn't get to talk

about my brother like that. "He didn't have a choice. He was suffering. You of all people should understand that." Jesse and I had never talked about this. "Why are you even saying this?"

In a rare show of temper, he threw his arm out. "Look at this place, Liv. You have a college degree and more intelligence than any woman I know but you're throwing it all away, walking dogs for a living and selling everything to get a nonprofit off the ground that glorifies what your brother did!"

"Leave," I ground out. "*Now*."

He stormed to the door. "Maybe you should ask yourself why I never kissed you before."

I wanted to tell him to fuck off but instead, I did something much worse. "Maybe if I'd enjoyed it, I would. But I didn't." Asshole Alex was right. Jesse *didn't* have any game. "Maybe you should've put a little more dick into it!"

He was on me so fast, I never saw it coming. One hand gripped a handful of my hair, the other grasped my face and Jesse kissed me, *really* kissed me.

My back hit the wall, his mouth slammed over mine and everything he didn't do in our first kiss, he did now. Aggressive and hot and consuming, he ground his hips against mine and he dominated me.

But it was all wrong.

And it was over before I could make heads or tails of what was happening.

"You want more dick? I got plenty. I'm just not an asshole about it." He walked out.

I slid down the wall and my head started to pound, literally, until I realized it was someone banging on the door.

"Go away." I didn't have the energy for this.

"Open up."

"You managed to get in all by yourself before. You figure it out." Fuck Jesse and his kiss. My head hurt.

The door swung open but I wasn't looking at construction boots… I was staring at Ferragamos. My gaze dragged up the length of his perfect fucking suit pants and landed on a tensed jaw. "Shit."

Alex scowled. "Your boyfriend left you like this?"

"I told you he's not my boyfriend." Why the hell did this asshole need to be so fucking hot? "Go away."

"Get up," he snapped

I didn't move. "Who the hell died and made you boss? Leave."

He didn't hesitate. He reached down and plucked me up, just like he'd lifted Mrs. Pendleton off my boss. "Where's the bathroom?"

I told myself I didn't bother squirming because I didn't have the energy, but in truth, he just smelled so damn good. "Put me down." I needed to remember he'd ruined my life. And fucked me. Royally.

"You walked home barefoot," he stated, like he couldn't believe it.

Well, that answered one question. "You followed me?" I should've been pissed, but I wasn't. I was being carried through my apartment like someone gave a damn about me and I was stupidly thinking how nice it felt. Fucking alcohol.

"You left your phone." He pushed the bathroom door open with his foot and set me on the toilet. "You need to put a lock screen on it." He turned the shower on.

I stared up at him. Somewhere between here and the

penthouse, he'd lost his jacket. His biceps straining his dress shirt, the sleeves rolled up to reveal ropey veins and his expensive watch, he looked more than capable. He looked determined. And he'd ruined my life. "I'm supposed to hate you."

"I get that." He adjusted the temperature.

But I didn't hate him. I was relieved. I didn't have to get up tomorrow and walk yippy little dogs or kiss my bitchy boss's ass or check fifty thousand details for a startup charity. I no longer had to sell my soul to pay a wager on guilt I'd never afford. Fate had walked into my fundraiser in an expensive suit and that was that.

Tendrils of steam filled my small bathroom and my thoughts bled into words. "I'm not admitting to shit, but if I were, I'd tell you I feel relieved. Do you know what kind of pressure I've been under?" Pressure not to fail. Pressure to start the charity. Pressure to do everything, every day, by myself. But now I didn't have to. I didn't have to do anything. I was at ground zero. I couldn't fail anymore.

"No." He tipped his chin at my dress. "Take it off."

"Planning a fundraiser is like a twelve-month root canal. And no way, I'm not falling for that again." I shook my head and slid off the toilet but he caught me just before my ass hit the tile. "Bad shit happens when I take my clothes off around you."

He smirked. "You're the first woman to tell me that."

I pointed at him. I think. "You're bad juju." *Fuck.* "Now I sound like Franklin."

His eyebrows drew together. "Who the fuck is Franklin?"

"The Cecile punching bag." I snorted. "I think I like Cecile."

"Don't get any ideas, sweetness. Submissive suits you." His hands around my waist, he lifted and I was on my feet. "Arms up."

I raised my arms. "Don't think for one second that I'm submissive." I swayed. "Because I'm not."

"Right." His sarcasm-laced tone said he didn't believe a word I was saying.

He whipped my dress over my head and my mind jumped. "You did, you know."

He blatantly scanned the length of my body and shook his head. "Damn, sweetness. Turn." He didn't wait for me to comply, he turned me. "What'd I do?"

"You single-handedly took down my fundraiser." Yeah, my boss had gotten all her little friends to withdraw their bids but Alex had pissed her off. I didn't think for a second it was just because his date had slapped her. "I should be impressed. One man with all that sway over so many women?" Most of the attendees tonight had been women. I'd chalked it up to women loving dogs more than men, but what the hell did I know? "Oh, no doubt about it, you're gooood."

"You have no idea." He unhooked my bra and slowly brushed his hands over my shoulders. "But I can't take all the credit on this one." His jaw clenched.

"I hate my fucking boss." I laughed but it didn't sound funny. "Wait. She's not my boss anymore. She *fired* me." I'd never been fired. "And who the fuck is she to fire *me*? I didn't get in a catfight over... over...." I looked up at him. "I don't even know your last name."

"Vega."

I snorted. "Not Vegas."

"No. In you go." He effortlessly lifted me into the shower.

Hot spray burned my chest. "Ow!" I scrambled to adjust the temperature.

His hand closed around my wrist. "Leave it."

"Why are you doing this?" I whined like a little girl then cowered in the corner farthest from the spray. I never whined.

He pulled me back and tipped my head to wet my hair. "Because you're dirty."

"You're dirty," I accused.

"I didn't walk six blocks barefoot," he calmly stated, running his hands through my wet hair.

"You fucked a stranger." Score one for me. Wait. *Damn it.* I did the same thing.

His chuckle was more ironic than humorous. "Wasn't the first time."

Something nudged at my brain, like a big giant clue I should've been picking up on, but it was as if all the vodka and whiskey had put a wet blanket on my reasoning. "You should be more careful." Did it count as fucking if I didn't come? "I could have a disease."

"As tight as you were? I doubt that, sugar." He plucked my shampoo bottle out of the caddy.

"What the hell does that mean?"

"Exactly as I said it. You're tight." His hand slipped between my legs. "There's no one tending this garden." He stroked me once.

My head fell back and my mouth opened on a moan and every nerve that'd been aching for release stood up at attention. He brushed his thumb over my clit then retreated.

"I hate you," I whispered.

"You want me." His strong hands massaged shampoo into my hair.

"You wish." Denial. Denial was safe... Jesse was safe. I groaned and slid down the wall. I wanted to crawl in a hole and never come out.

"*Hey.*"

He reached for me but I swatted him away. "Go away. I'm done with you." I curled into fetal position with my back to the spray and closed my eyes.

"We need to rinse you off."

"I don't care." I didn't care about anything, except the gnawing bite of embarrassment in the pit of my stomach. The fundraiser, Jesse, the man with the biggest cock I'd ever felt—I shivered and for three heartbeats, I felt utterly alone. Then the shower curtain slid back and arms wrapped around me.

"Come on, sweetness, on your feet. Almost done."

I was standing and cradled by a hard male body before I could open my eyes. I reached back for purchase and my hands encountered rock-hard muscular thighs. "You're naked."

His giant cock pressed into my back. "That's the idea behind a shower." He tilted my head under the water and rinsed my hair.

I looked up at him. Square jaw, hair wet and slicked back, his eyes the color of the ocean at night, he was even more handsome than in the penthouse. "Why are you here?"

"You left your phone." The words fell out of his mouth too quickly.

I turned in his arms. "You're lying."

His intense gaze zeroed in on me and the shower shrunk to two bodies caught between the hot spray and steam. He didn't deny it and I didn't push. My arms went around his neck and his hand cupped my face as naturally as if we knew more than this moment between us.

"Alex." I tasted his name, letting it slide past my tingling lips.

His thumb swept across my cheek.

And suddenly, everything caught up with me. I was in my shower, naked and alone with a strange man who didn't have blond hair or big brown eyes. I dropped my arms. "You were wrong."

"About?"

"Jesse kissed me again. He can put everything into it."

His nostrils flared but his voice remained steady. "Then why isn't he here?"

"He walked out."

Alex's chest rose on an inhale as his fingers worked their way through my wet hair to my head. "You're beautiful. You don't need him."

"You don't know me enough to know what I need." I was proud I'd strung all those words together without missing a beat.

This time, it was his cock that rubbed between my legs. "Don't I?"

I forced my muscles to hold still. "Sex doesn't solve everything." But sex with him? The way he was consuming me? How my nerves were hovering on the edge? I knew it would make me forget everything, at least for awhile.

He gently pushed me against the wall then bent his knees slightly. "Good sex does." Thrusting his hips up, he gave me more pressure.

Every lick of desire he'd ignited in the penthouse returned tenfold and I groaned shamelessly. "I'm not…." Oh my God, I wanted him. "I'm not fucking you again."

"I'm going to make you come."

Except he didn't say it like it was a given. He growled it like a warning and I should've known to push him away.

Because in the next second, he sank inside me and I lost all my resolve.

NINE

Alex

I HAD TO KNOW.

Just once, I had to know what this woman felt like without a condom.

And goddamn she was perfect.

But I was so motherfucking stupid. I slid halfway out of her tight heat then shoved right back in. She was so damn intoxicating, I couldn't catch my breath. Wet hair, water-slicked skin, hard nipples, she was fucking gorgeous. Gorgeous in a way I didn't want to think about.

I knew I'd ruined her fundraiser. Baiting that client had been a mistake. Shit, going in the first place had been a mistake. But I'd bought all the damn paintings, and now I was balls deep in the sweetest woman I'd ever felt. I didn't have an ounce of regret. If that's what it took to get me here, I'd do it a thousand times over.

I hitched her legs around my hips and latched on to one nipple then the other, and she unraveled in my arms. She wasn't falling apart because she knew who I was or what I was paid for. She wasn't getting off on some fuck fantasy of a male prostitute. It was just me and her and I wanted to come inside her more than anything I'd ever fucking wanted.

I bit and sucked my way up her neck, grinding my hips against her clit as possessive bullshit crawled up my consciousness and lodged in my chest. "You on the pill, sweetness?" Jesus fuck, I had no business asking. I needed to pull out and put on a goddamn condom. I'd never come inside a woman. Ever.

"No," she panted.

Fuck.

"Implant." She lifted her arm to show me, then arched her back and pushed down on my cock.

I kissed her.

Deep and heavy, my tongue sank into her mouth and I devoured her untainted pureness. Stroking in a rhythm that matched my thrusts, I wanted all of her. The taste of her lips, the feel of her coming on my cock, the look in her eyes when she let go. I wanted her for her and I made a decision.

I pulled back just enough for her to look at me. "I'm clean."

Her sexy, hazy, blue-eyed gaze met mine.

She looked so innocent, shit kicked at my chest from the inside and I needed to make sure she understood. "I'm not wearing a condom."

She sucked in a breath. "The implant, I've never tested it. I've never let a guy...."

My heart rate spiked and I gripped her chin. "Your decision." Goddamn it, I wanted this.

She squirmed and her muscles tensed around me. "You're so big."

"You're handling it." Too fucking perfectly.

"Kiss me," she whispered.

I dropped my hand to her clit and rubbed as I plunged my

tongue back inside her mouth. Three thrusts and she started to come. Gritting my teeth, I pulled out and warned her. "You come on me and I'm gonna follow suit. You hear me?"

"No!" she cried out, reaching between us.

"I'm not denying you, sweetness. You need to tell me what you want."

She grasped my cock and I jerked in her hands. "Yes, please, please, please," she begged. "Fuck me. Come inside me."

I shoved back into her and sank to the hilt.

We both groaned and I fucked her exactly how I wanted to, without barriers.

Pounding into her, my tongue twisting with hers, I dominated her. I didn't think about a fucking thing except giving us both what we wanted. With the water beating down my back, her legs wrapped around my hips and her tight pussy gripping me, I started to lose it.

Her back stiffened and her thighs shook. "I'm gonna… *ohmigod.*" She gasped. "I'm coming."

I reached between her legs and pushed her over the edge. Pulsing, spasming, squeezing my cock like a vise grip, she fucking detonated. I thrust three more times and let go.

I came inside her.

I fucking came inside her.

And I immediately wanted to do it again.

She gripped my neck and rested her head against my chest. "Oh my God."

Goddamn, I was never doing that again… but *fuck.* Aftershocks swept through her body and unlike every other pussy I'd ever fucked, I didn't want to immediately pull out. I wanted to stay buried so deep in her shit that I was right there the second my dick was hard enough to start thrusting again. "You good?"

"I think you split me in two."

I'd heard that before but coming from her, it sounded like shit. I forced a chuckle. "You'll recover in time for your boyfriend to pull his head out of his ass." The thought of that prick even touching her now made me see fucking red, which should've been my clue to get the fuck out of there.

"I told you, he's just my friend."

Fucking great. "I don't care what you call him. He wants to fuck you." I'd talked about my client's boyfriends, husbands, other lovers while I was with them and I'd never given two fucks about it. I welcomed the comparison. It's what made me bank. But this shit with her? While my dick was still buried so deep I was bottoming out? *Fuck no.*

"Jealous?" She smirked.

"I don't get jealous." I didn't know who the fuck I was lying to.

I had every intention of getting the hell out of there. I didn't know what the fuck was happening and I needed to re-group, alone. But when I started to lift her off my cock and ease out, I felt my come inside her and my brain warped, completely fucking one-eighty *warped.*

This wasn't some cougar's mouth or repeat client's well-played pussy. I wasn't shooting my load into a condom and counting the money in my head. I was sunk inside a tight little cunt that'd never had anyone's come but mine and shit dangerously shifted in my head.

"Then what do you care if he wants to sleep with me?"

My life split in two. Before I came inside her. And after. Dark, light. Bad, good. Hell, hope. There was no in-between.

I didn't know if I was panicked or ecstatic. All I knew, I'd set her on her feet and already wanted back inside her.

"I said fuck, not sleep." But it didn't matter. He wasn't going to do either with her. "This sweet pussy?" I cupped her. "Only I get to come inside her." I staked my claim and damn, I was hard again.

She shivered. "I didn't agree to a repeat performance."

"Oh, sweetness." No way was I leaving now. Fuck giving that asshole a chance to come back tonight, or any night. I turned her. "Brace yourself, because I'm going to fuck you all night." I stroked her and my cock pulsed in anticipation. "By morning, you won't even remember his name."

She put her hands on the wall. "I'll never forget his name, I grew up with him." She pushed into my touch.

I got off on coating my fingers in our come and rubbing it up her ass. "But it'll be my name you scream when you come." Over and over, I dragged through our come and spread it around her tight little entrance. With just enough pressure, I drew a firm circle until the tip of my finger sank into her ass.

Her muscles clamped down on me. "Alex." Alarm tainted her voice.

"I got you, beautiful." I slowly worked my finger in a circle and put my lips to her ear. "Take a breath." Her body listened to me and my dick swelled. "Good girl. Let it out slow." She relaxed and my finger slid all the way in. "That's it, right there. You're gonna let me in, gorgeous." Two strokes in her ass with just my finger and I was ready to fucking explode. "You ever let anyone take this sweet ass?"

"Ohmigod," she panted. "No."

My eyes closed and I drew in a breath of pure fucking

possessiveness as I slowly stroked in and out of her ass. "Feel good, sweetness?"

"*Ohmigod.*" Her hips moved with me.

I sucked on her neck and my cock throbbed in anticipation. "I'm gonna make you feel so damn good." I eased a second finger in to stretch her and she jerked. "Breathe, beautiful, breathe." I reached around and shoved two fingers into her cunt before she could pull away, then I rotated until I found the spot I was looking for.

Her hips jerked and she pushed onto the fingers I had deep in her pussy. My second finger sank into her ass.

Fuck yeah.

"That's it, sweetness." I stroked her ass two more times then slowly pulled my fingers out and gripped my cock. I dragged the head through her wet pussy then pushed between her cheeks and centered against her ass.

"*Alex.* What are you doing?"

I bit her collarbone before I soothed it with my tongue. My fingers deep inside her, I increased the speed of my stroke. "Showing you what it feels like to be taken care of." I worked the head of my dick against her tightness.

"That's… oh God." Her ass pushed down on my cock and I sank inside an inch. "That's not my pussy. *Oh God.*"

Fuck, she needed to come so I could sink inside her. "My fingers are right on your G-spot, sweetness. You're gonna come without me even going near your clit." I increased the pressure of my hand and shoved my cock another half inch.

"*AHHHHHhhhhhh.*" She started to come apart.

"What's my name?" I growled, pounding my hand into her.

"Alex, *Alex….*"

I shoved my dick in her ass.

"ALEX!"

Jesus Christ. "This ass is mine." My heart pounding, my dick a rocket, I stroked the half of my shaft not buried in her and fucking exploded.

My knees locked, my muscles went rigid and the orgasm that'd built faster than a wet dream reared up and wrecked me. I came so damn hard, I kept pumping inside her. Seconds, minutes, hours, time ceased. I was in a fucking daze and this woman was every fantasy I never knew I had. Panting, I stood shell-shocked before I realized she was shaking, badly.

I reached and turned the water all the way to hot. "Hang on, baby." I wrapped my arms around her and pulled out as gently as I could. The second my dick left her ass, she whimpered.

"*Alex.*" Her voice hitched like she was going to cry.

"Shh, shh, it's okay. I got you, sweetness." I shut off the water and scooped her up.

Her head fell on my shoulder. "Hurts," she whispered.

Fuck. "Temporary, I promise." She was so fucking small, her pussy, her ass, her body in my arms. Goddamn it, I should've been more careful. I stepped out of the shower and set her on her feet but I kept one arm around her as I yanked a towel off the rack. Wrapping her up, I stared down at her giant blue eyes and emotions flooded my chest.

"I can't stop shaking," she whispered.

Jesus, she was beautiful. "Come on." I picked her up again. "Let's get you warmed up." I carried her into the only bedroom and yanked back the covers. Not letting go of her,

I crawled into the bed and pulled the comforter over us. Hit with her sweet scent, I turned her and brought her back to my chest. Then for a split second, I panicked. I didn't do domestic. I didn't do attachments. I didn't do emotion, *period.*

"My chest, it hurts."

Alarm spread through my veins and stripped all other thoughts. "Hurts how?" My training from the Marines kicked in, and I picked up her wrist to check her pulse. Fast, but not thready. "You breathing okay?"

"Yeah." Her voice was so small, she sounded like a child. "What's happening?"

Christ, I'd literally fucked her into shock. "You're okay, sweetness. You're going to be fine. Just relax. You'll warm up." I ran my hand over her shoulder and down her arm. "Even breaths." I coasted over her small waist and the swell of her hips. I repeated the caress a few more times and the shaking diminished. "That's it."

"I'm so tired."

"Close your eyes, baby." Every stroke along her curves made my dick twitch but I forced myself to ignore it.

Within minutes, her body melted into mine and her breaths evened out in sleep.

I let my head fall back on the pillows but three years of conditioning kicked in. I mentally cataloged the location of my clothes, the distance to my car and the miles to my penthouse. Thirteen minutes and I'd be home.

I didn't move.

Fuck my five-year plan. I closed my eyes and gave in to the contentment that'd lodged in my chest. I was almost asleep when she thrashed against me and cried out.

"No!"

"Hey." I stroked her arm. "You're okay."
She kicked at the covers. "*He's dead, he's dead, he's dead.*"
I cupped her face but her eyes were closed. "Olivia?"
She cried once more, rolled to her stomach and went
back to sleep.

TEN

Olivia

OH MY GOD, MY HEAD.
Ohmigod, I'd let him come inside me.
And shit. *Shit.*

I forced my eyes open and when I saw the other half of my bed empty, I exhaled. "Thank you, God."

"For what?"

Startled, I turned toward the sound of the familiar voice.

Jesse leaned on the doorframe. His arms crossed, he looked pissed as hell. "Get dressed. I need to talk to you." He disappeared down the hall.

Too late, I pulled the sheets up to my chin. Rolling over, I buried my face in my pillows and groaned. But the second I inhaled, expensive cologne and the memory of every inch of Mr. Wrong filled my head.

I glanced at the nightstand like there'd be a note or something equally chick-flick worthy. Cursing my stupidity and fighting a wave of nausea, I forced myself to get up and throw some clothes on. I put my hair up in a messy bun and shuffled toward the living room as I shoved all thoughts of Alex down and told myself I was glad he left.

I rounded the corner and ignored the six-foot-two construction worker I called my best friend. It was harder than it seemed, but my sights were on my one vice, and I needed a fix. Well, my one vice with the exception of last night. "I can't talk without coffee." Did a one-night stand count as a vice?

Jesse silently handed me a mug because he knew me. Because that's what best friends did.

Guilt spread through my chest and I muttered, "Thanks." I wasn't having a heart-to-heart or whatever he wanted to talk about without caffeine and he probably knew that, but it was still a nice gesture.

Leaning against the kitchen counter, his arms still crossed, he only nodded.

I took a sip and tension filled my galley kitchen. I refused to cower, but I also refused to look at him. I took three more sips before he spoke.

"You want to go first?"

Um, no. "Have at it." I steeled my nerves and gripped my mug.

"Jennifer and I broke up. I wouldn't have kissed you if I was with someone else."

Deep down, if I had thought about it, if I hadn't had five million other things going on, I would've realized this. Jesse wasn't that guy. But the information did nothing. Not to my heart, not to my ego. My pussy was achy and throbbing and I was consumed with dark hair and blue eyes and stupidly wondering if his number would be magically programmed into my phone. What should have been pure hatred for Alex was dangerously morphing into a fuck-my-life obsession.

"Liv?"

Would it be too obvious to go grab my phone to see? "I heard you." I needed to get a grip.

"Your turn."

I didn't know cocks came that big. "For what?" My last boyfriend lied to me. Size *totally* mattered.

Jesse exhaled. "Look at me, Liv."

I took a sip of coffee and peeked at him over the rim of my mug. For the first time in ten years, he looked like he could kick someone's ass. I mean, he was all hard muscles and imposing height, but he usually carried his strength with a smile. Not today. He looked so pissed, if I had room to, I would've stepped back. "What do you want me to say?"

He stared at me, really stared at me, and Jesse never stared. He was too polite.

"What happened last night?" His tone sharp, it wasn't a question. It was an accusation.

"What do you mean?" I hedged. Did he know about Alex? Did I care? Shit, of course I cared. This was Jesse. And he'd kissed me. Twice. Except I could hardly remember what that kiss felt like because I was thinking about a giant— Oh my God. I needed to stop.

"All the paintings sold to the same person."

I blinked. "What?"

"They're in my truck. Delivery instructions are for today." He reached into his back pocket and tossed something onto a kitchen chair. "Take a shower. I'll wait downstairs."

"Wait." I stared at the chair… and my underwear from last night. "How do you know this?"

"The buyer left instructions with the doorman." He walked out, slamming the door behind him.

Shit.

Well. At least I had my matching set back. I snagged the red lace thong off the chair and shuffled to the bathroom. I turned the shower on and stripped, but the second I stepped under the hot spray, I was reliving the best sex of my life. Just thinking about it made need rear up and kick me in the lady parts. I thought about an extra-long shower to get myself off and the satisfaction of making Jesse wait was icing on the cake. He hadn't even bothered knocking this morning. Didn't I tell him to cut that shit out last night?

Why was I even thinking about this? I should be jumping for joy that I sold all the fucking paintings. But I wasn't. I was tired and horny, and I wanted a stupid repeat with an asshole who'd snuck out in the middle of the night so he didn't have to ever see me again. Issues didn't begin to cover what was wrong with me.

Twenty minutes later and no shower-gasm, I yanked open the door to Jesse's truck and hopped in with a fresh dose of attitude.

Jesse had the truck's AC cranked to nipple cold, his phone was to his ear, and he had a distracted look I knew well. He didn't even glance at me. Looking far too capable, he pulled into traffic as his muscles stretched the sleeves of his T-shirt.

For five blocks, I stole glances at him and wondered if our friendship would ever be the same again. By the time he'd hung up, my mind was spinning and my mouth opened to spit out my fractured thoughts. "You're moving hours away." What the hell did he think would happen when he kissed me last night?

"You could move too." As if he hadn't just thrown my dirty sex underwear on my kitchen chair, his response didn't miss a beat.

"You want me to come with you?" He made this

decision hours after dumping his girlfriend? And seriously, we were actually going to talk about this?

"Yes." Again, no hesitation.

My eyes narrowed. "You're not looking at me." And that felt purposeful.

"I'm driving."

"No, there's more than that." I knew him. I knew when he was hiding something.

He abruptly pulled over, threw the gear shift in park and yelled, "I kiss you and you go sleep with someone else?"

I sucked in a breath. Jesse had never yelled at me.

"Was it payback? You were pissed I dated Jennifer? I never even slept with her!"

My mouth popped open.

"What?" he demanded. "You're surprised? Shocked? Maybe I didn't want to fuck her."

Oh my God.

"I've been waiting two goddamn years but you don't ever seem to come out of it. Your brother's dead, Liv. He's not coming back. You deserve a life. *I deserve a life!*"

Everything from the night my brother died came rushing back. Jesse had taken me to dinner. He'd just gotten out of the Marines. He'd been stationed all over and with the exception of a few rushed visits, we'd kept in touch with e-mail and texting, and I'd missed him. I was so happy to have him home, but he'd been quiet. He'd stared at me over dinner and I'd thought for sure he was going to finally kiss me that night. But then my cell phone rang and everything changed. "Jesse," I whispered.

He shook his head. "I was going to kiss you that night," he said, as if reading my thoughts. "I wanted you, Liv. I wanted everything."

Wanted. Past tense. "And now you don't." Something raw and gnawing churned in my stomach.

He ran a hand through his hair and his voice went back to its usual quiet calm. "I don't know what I want."

Guilt. Regret. They were there but something was building. Something a whole lot like anger. "So you dated Jennifer because you wanted me?"

"Don't turn this around."

Really? Turn around the fact that he was dating someone and I wasn't? "How exactly am I turning it around that you had a girlfriend all the while you 'wanted me'?" I couldn't stop myself, I made obnoxious air quotation marks. "Because that's a seriously fucked-up way of showing me you *wanted me.*"

He stared at me. "This isn't my fault."

"So this is a *fault*? You not saying what you want? *I waited years for you to come home.*"

His nostrils flared with an inhale. "I never told you to wait," he bit out.

"That's just it, you never told me anything! You didn't tell me to wait for you. You didn't tell me you liked me. You didn't even tell me you wanted to kiss me. You've never even told me I was pretty!" But that asshole had. He'd told me I was beautiful. And goddamn it, I wanted to be beautiful to someone.

"What was I going to do? Call you from Iraq and tell you the only thing keeping me sane was a picture of you in your bikini?"

My heart crushed in on itself. I knew that picture. We'd gone to the beach before he'd deployed and I'd laughingly snatched his phone and taken a selfie. My tits pushed together, I'd made kissing lips and snapped the shot. I'd tossed his phone back at him and joked that he could add it to his spank bank. That was the last time I'd seen the carefree Jesse. He'd deployed and the next time I saw him, he was more reserved. He'd also put on fifty pounds of muscle.

"You should have told me." I refused to shoulder the weight of all of this. This wasn't all me.

Deep brown eyes locked on mine and he nodded. "You're right. I should have."

The sincerity in his tone, his eyes, it made the anger that'd been building morph into guilt and I just couldn't take on any more blame. "I can't apologize for last night."

"I can." He leaned toward me.

"Jesse," I warned, but he didn't listen.

He grasped my chin and came closer. "You're the prettiest girl I know, Liv. Always have been. I'm sorry I didn't tell you sooner." He released me then pulled back into traffic.

My head spinning, I didn't say a word. He drove in silence to one of the new high-rise condo buildings on Collins Avenue and pulled into the garage. He parked near the freight elevator and we wordlessly worked as a team, pulling all the paintings out of the truck and loading them into the elevator. I held the door while he parked his truck then we rode up to the penthouse level.

I hadn't bothered looking at my phone this whole time. I didn't want to know how much the paintings had sold for or to whom. I wanted to get this over with then I'd do what I'd been doing for two years. I'd throw myself into the work.

Jesse broke the silence. "You looked surprised when I said the paintings all sold to the same person."

"I was. You left before the drama last night."

He frowned. "What happened?"

"My boss got in a catfight with another donor over the date she'd showed up with. Then she fired me, left and took all the buyers with her." I held back the part about that date being Alex and how I'd gotten shitty drunk then fucked him. "Last I checked, all the bids had been canceled. When I walked home last night, I thought I hadn't sold a single painting."

Jesse turned completely to face me, his features twisted in shock. "Why didn't you say anything?"

I shrugged. "By then I was drunk."

The doors slid open and he pulled me in for a quick hug. Soap and familiarity wrapped around me and in the corner of my heart that craved stability, I wanted everything in the past twenty-four hours to be different.

"I'm so sorry, Liv."

His quiet voice touched my heart but unlike every other time he'd ever hugged me, it wasn't aching for more. "Not your fault. Let's get this over with." I pulled away and pressed the hold button on the elevator to keep the doors open.

He immediately picked up on my wording. "Over with?"

I shrugged again. "I don't know what I'm going to do. There are plenty of charities that train service dogs for vets. I could donate the money to them."

"You love animals," he reminded me.

"I'm tired, Jess." The confession hurt my heart almost as much as the thought of giving up.

"Come to Ocala with me."

Five words. Five words I would have died to hear a day ago. But today they felt uncomfortable and my smile was forced. "Let's get these unloaded then I'll buy you breakfast."

For a split second, something crossed his features but then he hid it and nodded. "Deal."

We worked in silence for a few minutes and when all the paintings were stacked against the wall by the door of the penthouse, I released the hold button and Jesse rang the bell.

A few beats and the door opened.

Shock didn't come close to what happened to my body. Because there wasn't a person on this earth I expected to see less than him. All six feet four inches of him. Muscles and a bulge in his jeans I knew all too well and the cockiest of grins that came from having a ten-inch dick you knew what to do with, Alex opened the door.

"Really?" I snapped. I should've seen this coming.

"Surprised, sweetness?" He didn't even bother acknowledging Jesse. He just raked his eyes over my body and lingered at my tits like he had a right to look all he wanted.

"Fuck you." I spun and grabbed two of the paintings, intent on the elevator.

"Liv." Jesse grasped my arm. "What's going on?"

Alex smirked. "Yeah, *Liv*. What's going on?"

I jerked out of Jesse's grasp and jabbed the elevator call button. "I'm not selling these paintings to him." He was not bankrolling my charity, no fucking way.

"It's a little late for that, sweetness. I already bought them. You wouldn't want my lawyer having a conversation with you about contractual obligations, would you?"

Of course the pretentious jerk had a lawyer. "I'm not obligated to you for anything."

Alex pulled his phone out and casually leaned on the doorframe as his thumb swept across the screen. "I'm paraphrasing here, but *all payments are final, no refunds, local delivery upon request,* seems pretty clear to me." He shoved his phone back into the pocket of his perfectly worn-in jeans. "Maybe we should ask your boyfriend." He glanced at Jesse. "Am I wrong?"

The elevator doors pinged open.

"Liv," Jesse's quiet voice reasoned, "wait for me down-stairs. I'll carry the paintings in."

Fuck, shit, damn. I knew what the wording in the bids said. I'd written it. I'd stolen the whole damn thing from some stupid template off the Internet. I knew it would come back to bite me in the ass but I never expected it to be because some jerk wanted to *keep* a painting. And hell no was I going to leave Jesse alone with Alex. Who knew what Alex would say to him.

So I bit my tongue, pivoted and walked right up to Alex. "Fine. Keep your paintings."

His stupid, fucking, cocky smile in place, he leaned back just enough to let me pass. "Those can go in my bedroom."

I took two strides into his fancy fucking condo and dumped the paintings against the entryway wall. "You carry them into your bedroom."

"Aw, and here I thought you'd want to see the view."

Heat hit my face and I made the mistake of glancing at Jesse. I could see the exact moment that he put two and two together and his expression morphed into sheer anger as his nostrils flared. Then his eyebrows drew tight and just like in the car, he locked that shit down and spoke in a calm voice. "Where do you want these?"

Alex sighed like he was put out. "The hallway, but don't scratch the paint on the walls."

What an asshole. Irrationally pissed, I carried two more

paintings in while Alex just stood there and watched with a smug look on his face. Jesse was silent but his jaw was ticking and more than anything, I wanted to lash out at Alex. Not for the paintings, but for leaving last night. And if that didn't spell f-u-c-k-e-d, then I don't know what did.

Jesse grabbed the biggest painting and placed it in the hall, and I followed with the two last smaller ones. Without even a glance in Alex's direction, Jesse walked out, and before I could follow him, Alex kicked the front door shut and caged me against the wall. His giant hands landed on either side of my head and he leaned toward me.

"What's wrong, sweetness? You pissed I left last night?"

"I don't give a shit what you do."

The side of his mouth tipped up. "Oh you little liar. Damn, that's sexy. What else you gonna fight me on?"

Jesse pounded on the door. "Liv!"

"I'm fine," I yelled toward the door. "Be right there."

Alex traced a finger down my arm and gooseflesh rose. "Will you?"

I jerked away from his touch. "Will I what?"

"Be right there." He ran his finger over my hip and ever so slightly down the inseam of my running tights. "Because I think you and I have unfinished business."

No underwear. I fought a moan and instantly soaked my pants. "Then I'll finish it. Go fuck yourself, you egotistical jerk. I don't need your money or you."

He smirked. "Really? Because—"

"You have two seconds, Vega. Open the door," Jesse boomed.

Alex's hand froze and he glanced at the door. "Now that's an interesting development."

ELEVEN

Alex

I RELUCTANTLY LET GO OF OLIVIA AND YANKED THE DOOR open. Bob the Builder looked fucking apoplectic. "How do you know my name?"

Ignoring me, he reached for Olivia. "Let's go."

Her eyes narrowed, her lips thinned, and I almost felt sorry for the prick. I'd seen the exact same look last night half a second before she let loose.

"Seriously?" she snapped at Bob. "You think I need *rescuing*?"

I leaned back to watch the show and Bob did what any prick who can't handle a feisty woman does. He retreated. All the way to the elevator and without a word.

"You didn't answer my question," I called after him.

He punched the call button and before he stepped inside the elevator, he spared me one infuriated glance. "NC Construction. I built your penthouse."

Damn. He was Bob the Builder.

The elevator doors started to close and Olivia kicked my front door shut.

"You ready to fuck, sweetness?" Just thinking about sinking inside of her had me hard. Shit, I'd been hard since

91

I'd left her bed early this morning but I'd had no intention of being there when she woke up. Not fucking happening. I knew the psychology of women and I was betting her beautiful ass wasn't any different. She'd either regret the shit out of last night or wake up wanting what wasn't there. Either way, I wasn't stupid enough to stick around and find out. I was playing my hand.

"No. And don't call me that."

"Then what's with the door slamming?" When I'd bought all the paintings last night and left instructions for delivery, it was on impulse. I didn't bring women or clients to my home. But now, after coming inside her tight cunt and seeing her here? I'd be lying if I said she didn't look hot as fuck in my place.

"I don't need to be rescued by you either. You want to keep these paintings, fine. But don't expect shit in return."

"Did I ask for something?" I was imagining every surface I could fuck her on.

"Call me a cab."

I took a calculated risk. "You call." I walked into my kitchen. "I'm making breakfast." I'd already eaten after my workout this morning, and it was too early for lunch, but fuck if I was going to tell her that. A thousand bucks said she'd woken up hard and I knew how to make a great fucking breakfast for hangovers.

I pulled eggs, potatoes, cheese and peppers out of the fridge. I was setting them on the counter when she walked into the kitchen.

"Where's your phone? I don't have mine."

"You have a bad habit of leaving it." I cracked eggs into a bowl and added sour cream.

"I hate phones. What are you doing?"

Hook, line and sinker. Chicks loved a guy who could cook. "Making you breakfast."

"I'm not hungry."

"You're ornery as shit, you're definitely *something*. And since I fucked you less than eight hours ago, I'm going with hungover. You're gonna eat, sweetness, so sit your ass down and pretend to be grateful." I whisked the eggs and turned a burner on.

"I'm not going to pretend shit and I don't owe you anything."

"Then stand. I don't give a fuck but one way or another, you're going to eat."

"Who the hell died and made you boss?"

I put the bowl down, closed the distance between us and tipped her chin. "Good question. Who did die?" The cries she'd made in her sleep last night weren't just a nightmare. I'd seen it too many times in the Marines. PTSD manifested in all sorts of fucked-up ways. There was a reason she was starting a charity for vets and I wanted to know what it was.

"What are you talking about?" She tried to shake my grasp but I held tight.

"Here's how this is going to work. You're going to drop the attitude with me. You're going to eat my food and you're going to be fucking civil about it. We're going to talk about whatever bullshit small talk you want then you're going to tell me why you're so goddamn defensive."

She scoffed but I could see the alarm in her eyes. "I don't need a daddy and I don't need some stranger's shoulder to cry on."

I picked up on her use of words. "There's a whole lot you

need but for now, we'll settle on breakfast." I dropped my grip and walked back to the stove. "Plates are in the cupboard. Set the table."

For three seconds, she didn't move. Then she shoved past me and threw open one of the cupboards. I didn't tell her she was on the wrong side of the kitchen because frankly, I was getting off on watching her throw a tantrum. Shit was definitely fucked-up in my head over this one.

She banged open three more cupboards before she turned to me. "Where are the plates?"

I smiled my panty-dropping smile. "Last cupboard on your left."

"Then why didn't you say so?"

She turned and I got a spectacular view of her ass. "You didn't ask."

"So I gotta ask all the obvious shit?"

"Ask whatever you want." Didn't mean I would tell her the truth.

"Why'd you buy the paintings? You don't strike me as the motivated by guilt type, even though you single-handedly ruined my fundraiser."

I wasn't sorry she was standing in my kitchen, so I didn't care how she got here. "We went over that last night, sweetness. I didn't *single-handedly* ruin shit. I'm not repeating myself." I told her the truth about the paintings. In part. "And I bought those paintings because veterans need all the help they can get."

"You're a veteran. You don't look like you need help."

"I don't. Did you serve?" I didn't think so, she had way too much attitude to ever cut it in the military, but stranger things had happened.

"No." She clanked my expensive dishes on the kitchen bar like they were Pottery Barn castoffs.

"Don't break my plates."

She picked one up and turned it over. "What kind of bachelor has Villeroy and Boch china?" She blanched and almost dropped the plate. "Holy fuck… you aren't married, are you?"

"Do I look like I'm married?" I sliced up the potatoes and threw them in the hot pan.

"Then why the hell do you have fancy plates like this? They're not even symmetrical."

Why did I have expensive anything? "Because I can. Come here."

Her eyes narrowed. "Why?"

"You're going to help."

"I don't cook."

I shook my head. "The odds aren't stacking up in your favor, babe."

"What the hell does that mean?"

"You don't cook, you don't do grateful, you're all attitude and you can't handle your alcohol." I glanced at her and tipped half my mouth up. "No wonder that pussy was so tight."

Heat colored her cheeks beautifully. "You're a pig."

"Yet I find you sexy."

"And you're demented." Her hands went to her hips like she was totally put out. "I'm not getting my hands dirty."

I laughed. "Oh yes you are. One way or another, sweetness, you're getting dirty."

"Do you think about anything besides sex?"

No. It was my business. But for some reason, standing with her in my kitchen, it wasn't something I wanted to talk about. Sex with her? Fuck yeah. But the back-to-back clients

I had booked for tonight? Hell no. "I'm thinking about why a hot brunette decides to do a charity for vets." I handed her the spatula for the potatoes. "Stir."

She took the utensil but she didn't say anything.

Damn, she smelled good. "You didn't have a dog at your place." I started grating the cheese.

"My building doesn't allow them. What is this, twenty questions?"

"I bought all your paintings, I think I'm entitled to a few questions."

She dumped the dirty spatula on the counter and pointed at me. "I knew there were going to be strings attached. You don't give a shit about veterans with PTSD. You just want to hold something over my head."

Shit clicked in my head. "Who was it?"

"Who was what?"

"Who died?" I watched her face for a reaction. "Boyfriend? Husband?" Nothing.

She dropped her hand and her challenging stare wavered. "What are you talking about?"

"Father?" It had to be someone she was close to. "Brother?"

She looked away.

Bingo. "Your brother."

With her back to me, I couldn't see her face, but I didn't have to. Her quiet voice was a dead giveaway. "I don't have a brother."

"I'm sorry." And I was. "What branch did he serve in?"

She exhaled and her voice went even quieter. "Marines."

"Iraq?" Jesus, I wanted to put my arms around her.

"Afghanistan. Three tours."

"Did he make it home?"

She nodded.

"But he wasn't the same." Fact of combat, it changed you.

"No." She pushed the single word out.

Her arms crossed over her body, her head down, you didn't need to be a genius to figure out what happened. "Stir the potatoes, sweetness. I'm done grilling you."

She didn't move and I seized the opportunity. I stepped behind her and wrapped an arm around her waist. Then I put the spatula in her hand, turned her toward the stove and helped her stir. "Why don't you cook?"

"I don't like it."

Her voice was so small, her grief was palatable. "Who doesn't like to eat?"

"I didn't say I didn't like to eat."

I chuckled to break some of the tension. "You want good food, you gotta learn to cook."

"There's only so many ways to pour hot water over ramen."

"Ramen's not food." I ate enough of that shit growing up and in the military that I never wanted to eat it again.

"Sometimes it's the only food you can afford."

"Then come to my place and I'll feed you better." Shit, I'd give her steak every night if she wanted it. "I can afford it."

She dropped the spoon and pushed away from me as she glanced around my penthouse. The attitude she usually threw out came back full force. "Nope, you're sure not hurting for cash, are you?"

I crossed my arms. "I bought your paintings, didn't I?"

"And dated my boss."

"I didn't date her." I didn't date any of my clients.

"Date, screw, fuck, whatever. Why don't you go back to your rich cougars?"

Goddamn it. "Because I'm exactly where I want to be." My defenses kicked in. "You got a problem with money, or only with people who have it?" I recognized the disdain in her eyes. I grew up in shithole like her place and knew what it was like to look at life from the outside. I never had a steady roof over my head until I enlisted. But everything she was looking at now? I fucking earned.

"Not one problem." She eased back a few steps. "You enjoy your paintings." She pivoted and walked to the front door. "See ya around."

Fixated on that heart-shaped ass in black spandex, it took me a half second longer to react. "Tell me one thing before you leave."

Her hand on the door handle, she paused and turned. "Yes, your cock is huge. Yes, I came a bunch of times. Yes, I enjoyed every second of it." Her voice turned drippy sweet. "And yes you were *the best* I ever had." She dropped the pretense. "Anything else?"

Fuck me. "Where do you train the dogs?"

TWELVE

Olivia

INFURIATING, THAT'S WHAT HE WAS. INFURIATING AND controlling and he got under my skin like no one I'd ever met. Fuck his sexy day-old stubble and jeans hanging low on his hips. I told myself I didn't care about his soft T-shirt stretched over his rock-hard abs. I just needed to get out of there before I did anything else stupid, like kiss him. Or sleep with him again.

"I was going to rent kennel space." I opened the door but before I could walk out, a large hand landed on it and pushed it shut.

"Going to?" His breath touched the back of my neck.

Gooseflesh spread across my skin and my pussy pulsed in anticipation. "I'm donating the money to another charity." It was easier than starting from scratch. And even if my bitch ex-boss would still rent kennel space to me, I wanted nothing to do with her or whatever past she had with Alex. I didn't even want to *think* about that.

"You're donating my money?"

"It's not yours anymore." There, take that, you arrogant jerk. Except, if I was being honest with myself, I'd acknowledge that he wasn't a jerk. He didn't have to buy all the paintings, he'd already gotten what he'd wanted out of me. But he'd bought them anyway. And he didn't strike me as someone who'd be ruled by guilt, so that left what? He'd bought them so he could see me again?

His hand landed on the back of my neck and strong fingers worked muscles I didn't know were sore. It was everything I could do not to sink into his caress.

"The money's for PTSD service dogs," he quietly reminded me.

"I know what it's for and it'll go to a charity that trains them." I didn't want to melt every time he breathed near me but my body wasn't listening.

He lowered his voice. "I want you to train them."

I stupidly looked over my shoulder. "Why?"

His deep blue gaze focused intently on me. "Because you'll be good at it."

Inhaling, I tried to not let the compliment find purchase. "Yeah? And what are you good at?" Besides fucking? "This penthouse didn't come cheap."

He smiled but it didn't touch his eyes. "My investments have paid off."

Cagey and aloof, I silently reminded myself, not dating material. Ex-boss revenge screw, catch and release, total player, do not get attached—I silently recited every damn reason I could think of to convince myself to walk away. "Great, good for you. Thanks for...." I glanced at the paintings in the hall and my traitorous heart constricted at the thought that this would be the last time I saw him. "Yeah, anyway, have a nice life." I needed to leave right now. And find Jesse. And apologize and get back to my old life. This fancy penthouse wasn't my reality, and every second more I spent in it, my brain twisted with dangerous thoughts of what-ifs. I yanked the door open

"*Olivia.*"

The command in his voice made a shiver dance up my spine and gooseflesh break out across my neck, but I wasn't falling for it. "Good-bye, Alex."

I walked out with as much dignity as I could because I knew his eyes were on me as sure as I knew what would be waiting for me in the garage. I stepped into the elevator that was bigger than my bedroom, and when I turned, he was staring.

"How are you getting home?"

"Jogging," I lied.

His gaze strayed to my legs then crawled back up my body. "I know a better workout."

"I'm sure you do." The door slid shut and I exhaled. "Holy fuck." I needed to get a grip. And a life. Jesse was right. I'd been hiding for two years and it was time to change that.

I rode the elevator to the garage instead of the lobby because I knew Jesse wouldn't leave me here without a ride home. At least, I didn't think he would. But by the time the doors slid open, I was down to thinking I had a fifty-fifty shot that he'd still be here.

Apparently, the odds weren't in my favor. His truck was gone.

Damn it, I really didn't want to jog home. I was a lot of things, but insane wasn't one of them. This was Miami and it was sunny, which meant it was only ten degrees cooler out than the surface of the sun. But no wallet and no phone meant no options.

I sighed and rode the elevator back up to the lobby and

told myself I was winning at life because I'd worn sneakers today. Sneakers that squeaked on the shiny travertine floors as I walked across a lobby that had more glass than my entire apartment building. It was also air-conditioned to a healthy arctic chill so that when I stepped onto the sidewalk, the difference in temperatures made me instantly soaked with sweat. Three blocks later, the humidity a hundred times more oppressive than usual, I was downright disgusting when an expensive sports car cut in front of me as I tried to cross a street.

My middle finger went up as the tinted window slid down.

Alex grinned at me. "That doesn't look like jogging."

"I'd tell you to fuck off but it has zero effect on you." It worked on everyone else, why the hell didn't it work on him?

"How about you just tell me to fuck you?"

A bead of sweat dripped down my back and joined its friends on my waistband. My hair was stuck to my forehead and my tank top was darker between my boobs because giant tits made special hiding spots for sweat. "If you were any good, I would. But you're not. So fuck off." Maybe if I kept saying it, it would pile up and stick.

He laughed. "Get in, babe."

"Do you know that ninety-nine-point-nine percent of women hate the word *babe*? It's a proven cockblocker."

"Never had a problem with it. Now get in the car before you have heatstroke, *sweetness*."

I wasn't getting in his fancy whatever-it-was car all nasty and sweaty. The last thing my ego needed was him smelling me like this. "Tempting, but no thanks. I'd rather take my chances than get in a car with a stranger."

He didn't miss a beat. "You know what happened last night?"

I was drunk, not passed out. Of course I knew what happened last night. I'd stupidly fucked him. Or he'd fucked me. Whatever. "You prematurely ejaculated?"

"DNA swapping. You know what that means?"

"I'm a crime scene?" My aching pussy sure felt like one.

"We're not strangers. Get in the car, because I promise, the alternative will be worse."

Not gonna lie, all the possibilities of his idea of an *alternative* had my mind running through a whole litany of scenarios, all of them X-rated. I shook my head. "Yeah, not happening." I pivoted and went the other way, trying to convince myself an extra block in my walk home was better than another roll in the hay with Mr. Wrong.

Thankfully, he didn't follow, and two blocks later, I was wondering just how insane I really was for giving up an air-conditioned ride, when footsteps came up rapidly behind me.

Normally I wouldn't have given it a second thought, but no one was out walking in this heat and the hair on the back of my neck rose as if my body knew who was coming.

"Like I said, sweetness, that isn't jogging." Alex passed me then ran backward as he delivered his comment. Running shorts, shirtless, more muscles than looked humanly possible, he grinned. "Come on, you're picking up the pace." He came to my side and nudged my shoulder. "Let's see what you're made of."

"What?" *The hell?*

"One foot in front of the other. Pretend you're running from me if it helps." Not even out of breath, he chuckled.

Where the hell were his jeans? And his car? "You're stalking me now?" Was I flattered? Was all the money he'd spent on the paintings a warning I needed to get a restraining order stat?

"Making sure you get home safe. Come on, sweetness, let's jog this out."

He wasn't even sweating. What the fuck was that about? Did serial stalkers not sweat? And why was his body so goddamn *perfect*? "No."

Before the word left my mouth, he picked me up. Except he didn't just pick me up, he tossed me over his shoulder, fireman style, and slapped my ass. "You jog or I carry you."

Holy shit. "Put me down!"

"You gonna jog?"

"No!"

He slapped my ass again and started walking. "Then I'm not letting you down."

Sweating all over him, my ass jiggling in the air, I caved. "Fine! Put me down. I'll jog!"

He didn't put me down like he picked me up. Oh no, the fucker grasped the back of my legs and let me slowly slide down his bare chest and feel every stupid ridge of his model-perfect abs. Showing me his blinding white teeth and show-stopping smile, he set me on my feet.

If he breathed near my lady bits right now, I'd come. "I hate you."

He winked. "You want me."

That too. But I still gave him attitude. I yanked my hair out of my ponytail, redid it into a bun then put my hands on my hips. "Where's your car?"

"Parked in my garage."

"You drove back, changed, then jogged to catch up with me?" Definitely stalker material right there.

He grinned. "You didn't make it very far."

Him and his stupid smile. He didn't even look like the humidity was bothering him. I hated him more. "I'm just getting started. Think you can keep up?" I didn't know why I was egging him on, except everything about him brought out the worst in me. That is, until he touched me, then I was just a pathetic heap of wanton desire, ripe for the taking. My only choice was no more touching. I turned and started jogging.

"You gonna warm up, sweetness?"

"I'm already warm." Between my legs and everywhere else. But nothing was going to reduce my hatred of all things exercise. I'd taken up jogging three years ago and I still hated it with a burning passion. Almost as much as I hated his smug expression as he matched my stride.

He casually glanced around us. "Where's your boyfriend?"

"He's not my boyfriend, but ask one more time and it'll make me change my mind." Another half block and I wouldn't be able to speak, the humidity was that oppressive today.

He laughed. "Is that a threat?"

I grunted and tried to pretend I wasn't dying.

"Do you really think it's a smart move to piss off your charity's main supporter?"

"I don't owe you anything." But I kinda felt like I did, and I kept thinking about his stupid comment about me being good at training dogs. I was. I was great. But the only other person who'd ever told me that was Jesse and he didn't count because he'd said I was throwing my life away. Not even my mom encouraged me to pursue this. I'd spent so long telling myself it was the right thing to do, I no longer knew what was right. Or wrong apparently. I glanced at Alex. "Return the paintings, get your money back."

"Nice try. And for the record, I'm a little pissed about the Cecile painting. That would've looked great in my bathroom."

I stopped jogging and put my hands on my hips.

He went two more strides before he halted and came back. "Problem?"

"Why are you here?"

He grinned. "I have a proposition."

THIRTEEN

Alex

I'D THOUGHT ABOUT THIS ALL OF TWENTY MINUTES, BUT every successive minute, it made more sense. I was either losing my mind or dangerously close to becoming a pussy-whipped male escort. Either way, I'd convinced myself this was all about a tax shelter and not three years' worth of burnout. Or worse.

I smiled my money smile. "We'll partner on your charity."

Her eyes closed for a second and she sighed. "Fuck."

My smile faltered. "You got a better offer?"

"I knew you were too good to be true." She dropped her hands from her hips. "No one fucks like that and is normal."

"And Bob the Builder is *normal*?" That fucker left her without a ride or a phone. Twice.

"You don't even know me." She shook her head and muttered, "You're batshit crazy." She started walking away.

"I'm offering you money." What the fuck was wrong with her?

"I don't want your money."

"Hey," I barked, suddenly pissed. "I bought those paintings. I gave you capital. Why the hell are you walking away?"

She pivoted and her tits bounced as she stomped her

sexy ass right back to me. "You think you can throw money at whatever flavor du jour suits you and the world's just gonna be *grateful*? What do you even know about charities? Wait. Let me guess. You read in some financial magazine how it'd be a great tax write-off." She scoffed. "I don't need *or* want a partner, especially someone like you."

I ignored the spot-on tax write-off comment. "You're making a mistake." It was the first stupid shit that came out of my mouth. I was staring at her lips and wanting to kiss her so fucking bad, I was getting a semi standing in the middle of South Beach.

"Seriously? *A partner*? What are you gonna do? Clean up dog shit and hose down kennels?"

Hell no. "I'll hire someone to—"

She threw her hands up. "Who the hell do you think that someone is?"

Fuck this. I stepped into her personal space, grabbed the mess she'd made of her hair, and tipped her head back. "You're sexy as hell when you're pissed."

Her nostrils flared but her body bent toward me. "Let go."

"No." I held her gaze. "Go out with me."

For three heartbeats, she stared at me. "That's why you bought the paintings."

It wasn't a question, it was an accusation and I wasn't going to acknowledge it. "Dinner, tonight." I had back-to-back clients booked. It was easily a fifteen-grand night and right in that moment, I couldn't care less.

"No." She swallowed and her legs pressed together.

Sweet fucking victory. She may have said no but her body was telling me everything I needed to know. I fought a grin and touched my lips to her temple. "I'll pick you up at eight, beautiful." Then I forced myself to release her and step back.

"Alex." She stood perfectly still. "Wait."

"Eight o'clock." I winked then jogged away. Before I hit the corner, I glanced back to see her still standing there. A stupid grin spread across my face.

High on the thought of getting her under me again, I breezed through five miles and made my way back to the penthouse. The cardio should've kicked some sense into me but all I was doing was plotting. I made the first call before I hit the shower.

Sounding out of breath, Jared picked up after the fifth ring. "What up, poser?"

"You booked tonight?"

"Is it Saturday?" he asked sarcastically.

"Clear your clients. You're gonna make fifteen grand tonight."

"Bullshit," he grunted and a woman groaned.

"Jesus Christ, are you fucking a client right now?" Had I taught him nothing?

"No," he growled low. "Ahhh, *damn*. Hold on." The woman moaned loudly. "That's it, baby, right there... fuck... fuck... *fuuuck* ... damn that was good." He exhaled. "I'm back. Not a client."

I shook my head. "You're still fucking for free?"

"Best kind of fucking," he countered. "What's going on tonight? I don't do bachelorette parties. Or any kind of party."

He hated crowds. Ever since the Marines, he didn't do a lot of things. Like crowds, Fourth of July, concerts, or even a movie theater. "No parties. I got three clients tonight."

"What's the matter?" He laughed. "Losing your stamina in your old age?"

I was only one year older than him. "Fuck no. I got a scheduling conflict. You're taking all three and I get thirty percent."

"Ten."

"Twenty."

He sighed and I heard a door close. "I'm not fucking your old-ass cougars for eighty percent."

"Define old."

"Fifties and shit."

My oldest client was forty. Ish. "Stop being a pussy. You're off by a decade and the second client tonight is young." And inexperienced. Jared would scare the shit out of her.

"She hot?"

"She pays five grand, what do you care?"

He laughed. "I don't."

"That's what I thought. And don't be an aggressive dick with her, she's shy."

"Aw, come on, Sarge. You know I can't hang with that shit. I'm not a fucking pussy."

Jared was anything but a pussy. His game was rough and his clients ate that shit up. I'd sent a few women his way over the years and they never looked back. "Just take it easy and don't scare the shit out of her."

"She should fuck a woman if she wants gentle."

I didn't care what she did when she wasn't paying me five grand to pound her missionary style. "Suck it up."

He chuckled. "Maybe I will."

Christ. "I'm texting you the details now. Stick to the

script and don't be late." Jared was notoriously unpunctual. "Let me know if you have any issues."

"I don't have issues."

I wasn't touching that. "Catch you tomorrow."

"Hey. What's the real deal? You haven't taken a night off in years."

"Business dinner." It wasn't a complete lie.

"You branching out?"

Me and Jared and one other Marine buddy had talked about this a few times. I'd turned them both onto what I was doing. None of us were prepared for civilian life but I'd adapted quicker. Jared was into rough sex and he took to the business but Dane was a different story. That fucker was huge and silent and scary as hell. He'd disappear for days, sometimes weeks, and I wasn't sure what the fuck he had going on. Twice he'd called me to take a few of his clients because he'd looked like he'd been hit by a truck. When I'd asked what happened, he'd passed it off as a rough day at the gym. Which was bullshit because we all went to the same gym and none of us could take him in the ring.

"Looking into a charity," I admitted.

Jared burst out laughing. "What kind of charity does a hustler front? The boyfriend experience for needy chicks?"

"Fuck you." But he was right. None of us broadcasted what we did outside our circle. I wasn't an idiot. I couldn't do this forever. I'd known going in that I needed an exit plan, and I had one. For two years from now. "It's for veterans."

"Since when do you give a shit about veterans?" Jared had no love for the military.

"I'm talking to you, asshole, aren't I?"

He chuckled. "Fair enough. What chick got you involved in this?"

"I didn't say a woman was involved."

"What restaurant?" he asked, so casually I didn't see the trap.

"Pietra's."

He laughed, hard. "You fucking dog, you're going on a date. Does she know how you pay the bills?"

Christ. "Just take care of my clients tonight."

"I do that and they won't want to come back to you," he taunted.

A few days ago, that would've bothered me. "Give it your best shot. I'll still collect my twenty percent."

"No way, one-time deal only. After that, I keep my earnings. Unlike you, I don't do charity. Later." He laughed and hung up.

I called Dane. He picked up on the third ring, but same as always, he didn't say anything.

"It's Alex."

"I know." His deep, quiet voice had no intonation.

I exhaled, wondering if this was a stupid fucking idea to call him, but he was the only person I knew who had a dog. "What do you know about PTSD service dogs?"

"Hunter isn't a service dog."

"But let's say you wanted one, would you train him?"

"No. He's a personal pet."

"All dogs are pets."

"Not according to federal law. Service animals aren't pets."

What the hell? "For arguments sake, let's say you wanted your dog to be your pet and a service animal, what would that be? A therapy dog?"

"Therapy dogs are used in hospitals or schools, or

disaster areas. They don't provide assistance for their han-
dlers. They're not the same as a service animal. They don't
have the same accessibility rights."

"Rights?"

"Legal access to any public place."

Christ, I didn't know this was so complicated. "So how
could you turn Hunter into a service dog?"

"I wouldn't. I'd declare him an emotional support animal. It doesn't require any special training."

"Then how do you train a service dog?"

"Pick the right breed, give them basic training, then custom train them for each individual based on their needs and
then adapt dog to owner."

You've got to be kidding me. "Every service dog is custom trained? How do you make money on that?"

"You don't. That's why charities do this."

I rubbed a hand over my face. "How long would it take
to train one of these dogs?"

"Don't know. Months at least."

My mind was reeling and I was beginning to see what
Olivia was up against. "How many would you train at once?"
She'd need more than rented kennel space.

"One. Maybe two."

Jesus. She couldn't even have pets in her apartment.
How was she going to swing this? "Then after they're trained,
you give the dogs away."

"Basically."

"All right, thanks. You gonna be at the gym tomorrow?"

"I'm not in town."

"Vacation?" I joked.

"No."

I waited but he didn't elaborate. "You ever gonna tell me what you're up to?"

"Need to know." He hung up and a knock sounded on my front door.

Thinking it was the mailman with a package, I swung open the door and cursed.

"Irina." With a fucking suitcase. "What are you doing here?"

FOURTEEN

Olivia

DRENCHED IN SWEAT, THIRSTY AND PISSED AT MYSELF for spending the entire walk back entertaining the idea of how convenient Alex's offer would be, I trudged up my stairs. And because my life was already one big suck fest, Jesse opened my front door.

"I was leaving you a note."

"Yeah?" I wanted to be pissed at him but I was too busy having heatstroke. I pushed past him and went to the kitchen. "What's it say? Sorry I kissed you and made you walk home, but you needed to learn a lesson?" I filled a glass with tap water and chugged it.

He leaned against the counter. "I'm not trying to teach you a lesson."

Yum, unfiltered City of Miami water. I probably just got some waterborne disease. This was what happened when you made no money and used what little you had to start a charity. You couldn't afford Evian. "We talked about the key."

"I've always had a key to your place."

"And I've never had one to yours. How convenient for you."

He exhaled. "You're angry."

115

I didn't want to fight with him, but it was like a switch had been turned and I couldn't get past being mad at him since he'd kissed me. "Gee, what gave you that impression?"

"Is this about us or him?"

He wasn't getting off that easy. "You tell me. You're the one who was leaving me a note."

He didn't bite. "What happened after I left?"

Because I was in a mood, I let my mouth go. "He put his dirty hands all over me and forced me to do untold things."

Jesse's jaw clenched and his hands fisted. "What happened, *Liv.*"

I sighed dramatically. "We argued, he offered to partner with me on the charity, and then he asked me on a date." Just saying it made me tired. And I was tired of being tired. And stressed out. And when did my life become more than a simple plan to train a few dogs and make a difference in a veteran's life? "I'm going to shower."

I didn't wait for a response. I stripped out of my tank as I walked down the hall because I couldn't stand another second in my nasty shirt, and if I was being honest, Alex did more for me than just fuck me. I was no longer shy in front of Jesse. Let him see what he'd missed out on. Not that it mattered anymore because I'd already been ruined by a ten-inch cock.

Just the memory of last night had me hot and bothered and I wondered when I'd turned into *that* girl. The one who goes all weak in the knees for the first man to give her an orgasm... or ten.

"You're bruised."

Startled, I looked over my shoulder.

His gaze locked on my naked back, Jesse stood in the doorway. "You like it rough."

It wasn't a question, and even had it been, I didn't have an answer. I'd never thought about what I liked before last night. The memory of Alex holding me down on the bar as he fucked the hell out of me flooded my mind and I shivered. "Close the door."

Ignoring my request, he stepped around me and turned the shower on. "You didn't have to go to someone like him. You could've come to me."

My heart started to race and I crossed my arms over my chest. "I don't know what you're talking about."

"Yes you do." He grasped my hair at the base and pulled the elastic gently out.

"Jesse," I warned. "You need to leave." Everything he was doing was making me uncomfortable because this wasn't him. My best friend didn't follow me into the bathroom and stare at me. And he'd never touched my hair.

He tested the water. "I wouldn't have left marks on you."

"Okay." I held my hand up. "You're crossing a line."

"Which line is that?" His gaze swept over my body. "Because after last night, I didn't think you had many left."

I slapped him.

My hand stinging, my heart hurting, I watched the red imprint color his cheek and shame seeped deep into my bones. Tears sprang and words stuck, thick and unmanageable on my tongue but I pushed out a response that wouldn't sink us further past the point of no return. "Get out."

He dropped his voice but his brown-eyed gaze that was full of intensity held steady. "I always wanted you." He walked out.

I sank to the edge of the tub and curled in on myself. "*Shit.*"

Steam filled the bathroom and my body shook. Adrenaline, regret, anger, it was a stew I wanted no part of. But the meat of it was what really scared me. Deep down, my sixteen-year-old self was begging me to run after him. She wanted me to chase the boy who'd enlisted in the Marines. She wanted me to grab his hand and sink into his arms and beg him to forget what I'd done last night. She wanted a breath of the life that could've been. She wanted her brother back.

But he wasn't coming back.

Tears slid down my face and mixed with the hot sting of shame as I stripped off my pants and stepped in to the shower. I scrubbed and I scrubbed, but nothing eased the ache of guilt. I'd denied my brother for Jesse. One split-second decision and I'd taken him away. *My own brother.* He was dead and I was here, fucking my life away.

I didn't realize I was sobbing until the water shut off and strong arms wrapped a towel around me.

"I killed him." The confession seeped out like an open wound.

Silent body heat cradled me and lifted. Jesse carried me into my room and placed me on the bed. He didn't speak. He didn't comfort. He did what he always did when I broke. He pushed the pieces together.

It was the closest to home I'd ever felt. But in that moment, it struck me. I wasn't home. I wasn't even comforted. I was cold and tired. Desperation bled into despair and the poison of my guilt leaked onto us both. "I kill everything. Me, my charity, us." I couldn't hate him for wanting Jennifer.

Jesse wrapped the comforter around me.

He should want someone else. I was no one. I was racing toward a certain existence that counted on nothing but regret.

He didn't deserve that. Jesse hadn't done anything wrong. I had. *For years.* "I'm sorry."

As familiar as if this was his bedroom, he opened the drawer on the nightstand and pulled out the bottle of prescription sleeping pills I never took unless he gave me one. Shaking one into his hand, he held it to my lips.

Like an obedient child, I took it and swallowed it dry.

He didn't crawl into bed beside me. He didn't offer any words of comfort. His eyes didn't even meet mine. He pulled the curtains shut and he did what he did best.

He walked out.

FIFTEEN

Alex

"**A**ren't you going to let me in?"

Jesus fucking Christ. "How do you know where I live, Irina?" I didn't move.

She pushed past me in a huff. "The Third." She set her suitcase next to the paintings and waved a dismissive arm through the air. "He does the background checks on everyone."

I'd set up an LLC and bought the penthouse through it. It wasn't completely anonymous but it should've stopped most people from finding me. "I'm coming back to that, but you're not staying here." It made me wonder who the hell her husband was.

"I did not sign a prenup and I have nothing to do with what the Third does. I did not tell him to background check you."

"Your shit with him doesn't have anything to do with me, Irina. I told you, we're done. And if you had nothing to do with it, then how did you get my address?"

"He kicked me out and I needed somewhere to go. What's the problem?"

Was she fucking serious? "You showing up here is the problem." And the fact that I'd come inside a hot, mouthy brunette last night who had me jonesing so bad for another taste it was all I could think about.

She waved her arm again and her accent got thicker. "Is temporary."

"Check into a hotel, Irina."

Petulant, she huffed as she sat on my couch. "I have no credit cards. He took them."

"Not my fucking problem." But even as I said it, I knew I would cave and help her in some way. I hadn't forgotten that she was my second client. I'd met her right after my first and only client at the time died of cancer. She'd given Irina my name and rate, which was higher than what she'd paid me. I'd always wondered if she'd secretly hoped we'd wind up permanent. She'd hated Irina's husband.

Irina flipped her hair over her shoulder. "Are you done?"

"Done what?"

"Throwing the temper tantrum. Are you done? Because I am thirsty. White wine is fine."

I took it back. I wasn't going to help her. I picked up my phone and called Dane.

He answered immediately. "Can't talk."

I ignored him. This couldn't wait. I needed Irina out of here. "How long are you out of town? I have a friend who needs a place to crash."

"Male or female?"

"The latter."

"You don't have female friends."

I glanced at Irina. "You're right."

Pause. "Client?"

"Former."

"Seventy-two hours." He hung up.

I gave Irina a warning glare. "I'm going to shower then I'm driving you to a friend's place. He's out of town. You can stay there for three days then you're on your own. And you're not coming back here."

"Whatever." She flung her leg over the side of the couch and gave me a crotch shot.

Of course she wasn't wearing underwear. "Don't try it," I clipped.

She spread her legs wider. "I try nothing."

"I'm not fucking you, Irina."

"Fine." She reached between her legs and dragged a finger through her pussy. "I will take care of myself."

Goddamn it. Familiarity, conditioning, my dick came to life. "That'll be a first."

"You want me," she purred, licking her lips.

"No, I want you gone." I walked to my bathroom and locked the door.

I rushed through a shower and shave and got dressed. By the time I walked back out to my living room, Irina was on my coffee table. Naked.

Her head hung off the edge like a porn star and I knew exactly what she was doing.

"I waited for you," she said submissively.

My dick finally caught up to my head and got with the program. With Olivia's curves on my mind, not one thing about Irina or what she was doing turned me on. I crossed my arms. "You're not sucking my dick. I'm not fucking you. And I'm not getting you off. We're done, Irina."

"*Please*," she begged.

"Get dressed."

"But—"

"Now," I barked.

She rolled to her stomach and put her ass up in the air. "I will be good."

"Twenty seconds," I warned. "Put your clothes on or you're out on your ass."

Slow, all attitude, she got up and pulled her dress over her head and stepped into her heels. "You are the ass."

"I didn't call you an ass." Fuck, why was I bothering? "Get your shit." I held the front door open.

As if she had all the time in the world, she hefted her purse and grabbed the handle of her suitcase, but she didn't walk out. She stopped in front of me, grabbed my junk and licked my neck like a fucking dog.

"No one does it like me." She squeezed my balls. "You will miss this."

I refrained from reacting because I knew her. You fuck someone every week for three years, you learn shit. She liked to taunt and push. She wanted me worked up then she'd turn submissive as shit and take what she had coming. Until last week, it'd worked for me. Now I saw it for what it was. Irina was all about the game.

But Olivia wasn't. And goddamn her ass was perfect.

I smiled at Irina because it was exactly what she didn't want. "I wouldn't be so sure." I wasn't gonna miss shit.

She left her suitcase at my feet and strutted to the elevator.

Letting her have her last indulgence, I carried her shit to my car. She was silent until I was pulling out of the underground parking.

"You met someone." It wasn't a question, it was an accusation.

"Don't confuse the facts. We were done the second you wanted more."

She crossed her arms over her small chest. "I ask for nothing."

"You didn't have to." I couldn't believe I used to find her attractive.

"So you think you see something that isn't there then you end it? You are crazy."

"We're not a couple, Irina. Never were, never will be. You were my client, nothing more."

She snorted out a huff. "You are different. Something has changed since last week."

I'd fucked for free and I'd liked it. "Nothing's different except you're no longer on my schedule."

"Then we will fuck without the money."

I smirked. "Because you have none? Not happening. Not even if the Third was still paying for it. Move on, Irina."

"I don't want to." She pouted like she always did when she didn't get her way.

"You don't have a choice." Fuck, I almost wished Dane was home so he could take her off my hands, but I wouldn't do that to him.

"I have choices. Many men want me."

Christ, I was not in the mood for this bullshit. I knew how to shut her up but I wasn't about to touch her. "Sit back and enjoy the ride." I turned on the stereo and drove northwest.

Dane lived way the fuck out on a property surrounded by so much uncut land, you couldn't see his fence unless you looked for it, let alone the turnoff for his driveway. I pulled onto the gravel and entered the code to his security gate. He'd given me all his codes, for his gate, his house, even the crazy-ass bunker he'd built a couple years ago. He'd said I'd need them *in case*, but he'd never said what that in case would entail.

I drove up and parked in front of what looked like a cracker house on steroids. Wood frame, steep-pitched metal roof, deep-shade porch on all sides, it looked old until you walked inside.

I cut the engine and a strong gust kicked at the car. "Come on."

Irina turned away from the door. "We are in the middle of nowhere. I am not staying here."

"You said you needed a place to crash? Here you go. You got three days." I got out and grabbed her suitcase from the back. Leaves swirling around my feet, I took the porch steps two at a time.

She quickly followed. "You can't leave me here. I can't even call for help. The nearest neighbor is miles."

I figured that was the point when Dane built the place. "You'll survive." She wouldn't need shit. Dane kept the place stocked for the apocalypse.

She glanced up at the sky. "It looks like it is going to storm. What will I do if the power goes out?" She looked around with disgust. "What if a bear eats me?"

"No bears, just bobcats and deer." And a whole shitload of snakes. "Stay inside at dusk and dawn when they come out to feed." I held back a smile. "And I'm sure you'll figure out how to light a candle if the power goes out."

She stomped her foot but the wind ate up the noise. "*Alex.*"

Christ, she was annoying. "Get your ass up here or find somewhere else to crash."

"You can't abandon me here." She crossed her arms like she had a choice in the matter.

"It's all I'm offering." I dropped her suitcase on the porch. "Take it or leave it but make up your mind quick because I'm booked tonight." I glanced at my watch as a bolt of lightning lit up the sky. "You got thirty seconds to decide."

She huffed but she gingerly walked up the stairs and peeked inside a window. "I can't see anything."

I entered the code into a keypad by the front door and the lock released, swinging the door open. "Have at it, princess."

"I am not a princess." She took one step inside the place.

No, she wasn't. She was a pain in the ass. "Happy now?"

She glanced around then sighed as if she was put out. "Fine. I will stay here."

I smirked. Dane's place may not have had ocean views but it was as nice as my penthouse. Every finish was high quality, and while I didn't go for the country look, he made it work. "The fridge is stocked, there's satellite TV and bookshelves full of books. Don't rummage through his shit and stay out of the master bedroom."

She glanced at the keypad on the wall. "There's an alarm."

I showed her how to use it and gave her my code. Dane could change it once she was gone. I glanced at my watch again. "I gotta run. Call me only if it's an emergency." I turned to leave. "Remember, three days then you need to find another place."

She caught my arm and gave it one last-ditch attempt. "You didn't have to drop me as a client."

I looked down at her pleading expression. *Yeah, I really did.* "Good-bye, Irina."

126

SIXTEEN

Olivia

THE POUNDING IN MY HEAD WOULDN'T STOP. OVER and over like a cruel joke. I was intent on ignoring it until my name was thrown into the mix.

"Olivia!"

Pound, pound, pound.

My body wrecked from the sleeping pill, it took two more minutes to realize someone was at my front door. Groggy, I got up, threw on a robe and opened the door just to make the pounding stop.

I forced my eyes to focus. Alex. In a suit. "What are you doing here?"

His gaze made a quick pass over my body and he frowned. "What's wrong?"

"Nothing." Not wanting to stand another second, I pushed the door shut, but I failed to make sure he stayed on the other side. I was halfway back to my bed when he caught my arm.

"What'd you take?"

The anger in his tone was more than I could deal with. "Fuck you."

"Right now, sweetness. Tell me what you're on or you're going in a cold shower."

127

I was too tired to growl at him. "Sleeping pill."

He helped me into my bed. "In the middle of the day?"

"Yeah." My head hit the pillow and I sighed in relief. "Go away."

"No." He stripped out of his jacket and shirt.

If I hadn't been half out of it from the damn sleeping pill, I was sure I would've been drooling over his abs. "What are you doing?"

"Taking care of you." He stepped out of his shoes and undid his pants.

My brain struggled for a response as I stared at his chest. "Shirtless?"

The side of his mouth tipped up but there was no humor in his eyes. He tossed his pants over the same chair as the rest of his clothes. "It's your lucky day." He pulled the covers back and slid into my bed. A muscled arm went under my head and my back hit his chest as he pulled me in close.

I didn't have lucky days. "I didn't invite you."

"We had a date." His voice rumbled from his chest and landed around me like the comfort of a familiar blanket.

The sensation was so foreign and intoxicating that my eyes fluttered shut. "I'm not dating you."

"Ah, ah, ah, you're not going back to sleep." He grasped my chin. "Eyes on me, sweetness." He gave me a slight shake.

"No." Damn it, I was tired. "Let go."

Piercing blue eyes stared down at me. "Why'd you take a sleeping pill?"

"I couldn't sleep." Why did this feel so intimate? Why did *he* feel so intimate? His hold on me, his stare, he was making me feel closer to him than I'd ever felt to anyone.

His grip held firm. "Wrong answer. Try again."

I didn't know if it was because of the damn pill or because he was looking at me, really looking at me like he gave a damn, but my mouth opened and stupid words spilled out. "I was upset."

"How upset?" he demanded.

At first I didn't get it. Most people would've asked why I was upset. The question, his concern, for a moment, I let my guard down. "I was crying and Jesse gave me a sleeping pill."

Every muscle in his body stiffened. "We're going to come back to that asshole giving you drugs, but right now, tell me why you were crying."

The truth tumbled out. "I let my brother die."

His arms tightened their hold on me. "I'm sure it wasn't your fault."

"Yes, it was." I choked down the lump in my throat. "The night he died? I should've been with him. He asked me to take him to the cemetery and I said no."

"Cemetery?"

"My father's grave. He liked to go there. And that night…." Oh God, this hurt. "I told him I wasn't going to go with him."

"Shit." The curse came out on an exhale. "You're blaming yourself."

"If I'd gone with him, he'd still be alive." It wasn't blame. It was fact.

He grasped my chin and forced me to look at him. "You don't know that."

I pulled away and laid out my ugly truth like I had a right to dump my burden on him. "He took his own life that night and I wasn't there for him like I should've been."

He cupped the side of my face and held my gaze. "Listen to me. You may think you could have stopped what was coming, but that die was already cast." He said it so resolutely, like he'd seen it too many times to count. "Even if you had been with him that night, there's no telling what he would've done the next night or the first opportunity he had to be alone. He didn't end his life because you weren't there with him that night. He ended it because what he saw downrange changed him. We all lived it, but some of us never came to terms with it. It's got nothing to do with what you did or didn't do."

Silent tears streamed down my face. "I should have helped him."

Anger contorted his features. "Jesus Christ, who the fuck is your support system? I'm telling you, you're not a licensed shrink with PTSD training. You don't know how many ways that shit can manifest. You never had control over this and that asshole you call a best friend should have told you that."

I looked away. "Regardless, he was my brother."

His thumb swept across my cheek. "He may have been your brother before you sent him off to war but he came back a Marine. Like it or not, that changes a man. Some are cut out for it, others aren't. That's the harsh reality of the military and I'm not going to sugarcoat it for you. But what you're doing, this guilt you're harboring? It's bullshit, sweetness."

Part of me wanted to rebel against his brutal truth but the other part, the desperate part, it didn't want to carry this guilt anymore. It wanted to reach for his words like a lifeline. But the guilt in even thinking he may be right, in even considering that I wasn't in some way at fault for leaving my brother alone that night, it was suffocating. "I don't want to talk about this."

"Fair enough, but know this. We aren't responsible for other people's actions."

"Mm-hmm." I was afraid to look at him because I was afraid he was right. And if he was right, then that meant I couldn't have stopped my brother. But that reality felt like a crushing blow I wasn't prepared to deal with.

"Hey." He threaded his hands into my hair and waited until I was looking at him. "I'm sorry about the fundraiser."

I drew in a deep breath and tried to shove everything back down in the tight confines of my chest. "Is that why you bought all the paintings?"

He stared at me. "No."

"Then why?"

A flash of emotion passed across his face then he untangled his hands from my hair and pulled me back to his chest. "Because I could."

Alex and I may have been strangers, but I'd had two men in my life who'd come home from war a different person, and I knew the look in his eyes just then. And for some reason, it made me feel closer to him than I'd ever felt to anyone. We all had our demons but Alex didn't make me feel like I needed to have all my broken pieces pushed together. He made me feel like they didn't matter. That kind of acceptance was the only explanation for what I let bleed out of my mouth next. "I didn't go with my brother to the cemetery that night because Jesse asked me to dinner."

His only reaction was the slow stroke of his hand down my arm.

"I never thought I would say those words out loud, not to anyone," I admitted. "Jesse had just gotten home and I hadn't seen him in months. I didn't want to go with my brother to my Dad's grave just to watch him sit there in silence for hours. I was being selfish. I wanted to go with Jesse, so I went." I choked on a sob. "That night, my brother aimed a gun on himself as he sat on my father's grave."

Alex's lips coasted over my forehead as his arms held me with a strength I wasn't used to. "Jesus Christ, sweetness."

"I never told anyone about my brother and the cemetery, but I should have."

"You're telling me now."

"I could have stopped him." I should have been there for him.

I felt him shake his head. "He made his decision before that night."

"But he'd reached out to me, he'd asked me to go with him."

Alex turned me in his arms and gently, as if he were afraid of scaring me off, he brushed my hair from my face. "Did he carry a gun?"

"He had a concealed carry permit." A lot of people in Florida had them.

The backs of his fingers on my cheek stilled and his gaze, unwavering and sure, anchored me. "He was planning it."

If he'd been planning it, then maybe I could've stopped him. If it was a spur of moment decision made out of despair, then maybe I wouldn't have made a difference. I didn't know which was worse.

Alex cupped my face. "You can't live your life feeling responsible. That's a one-sided fight and the only person who's gonna lose is you."

I knew he was right but I rolled back over. It didn't escape my notice that not only was this the first time I'd ever talked about this to anyone, but I wasn't a hysterical sobbing mess. "I'm tired." And I was, bone tired, but a thread of something that felt like healing settled in my heart, and it had everything to do with the strong arms that held me to his chest.

"Almost done talking." Slowly, rhythmically, he stroked my arm again. "Tell me why that asshole gave you a sleeping pill."

"He's not an asshole." My defense of him was instant and automatic, but as the words came, I wondered why Jesse had done what he'd done.

"If his answer to you being upset was to drug you, then he's more than an asshole."

"He's tired of dealing with me." But Jesse never really dealt with me, not like Alex just had. Jesse and I had never spoken about my brother before this morning. I'd lost it when I'd found out he was gone and I'd cried for a week straight. I still cried, but actually talking about my brother with Jesse? It didn't happen.

"You call that a best friend?"

I didn't know what I called Jesse anymore. It felt like I'd lost him too, but with Alex's arms around me, it was hard to even be upset about it. "I'm done talking."

Alex pushed me to my back and rolled. His knee moved my thighs apart and he settled between my legs. Boxing me in with his arms on either side of my head, he put just enough of his weight on me to make me feel safe. "You are not responsible for your brother's death."

A tear slid down my cheek.

"Say it," he demanded.

More tears fell. "I'm not responsible." I selfishly wished I'd had him in my life when my brother died.

Fierce determination sharpened his features as his strong hands gripped my hair. "Believe it."

For the first time in two years, hope spread through my chest. "I want to stay right here… in your arms," I whispered, exposing my heart.

His nostrils flared and, for one desperate moment, time stopped. His eyes, the color of the deepest part of the ocean, stared at me as if he saw every ugly truth I tried to hide from. His breaths measured, his heart beating against my chest, he didn't say a word.

Regret ate at me and I closed my eyes. "I'm sorry. I didn't mean—"

His lips landed on mine.

Searing and consuming, he thrust his tongue into my mouth and kissed me.

But this wasn't a kiss like last night. His hands pulled my hair, his cock thrust against my entrance, and he delved into my mouth like he needed me to breathe.

Desperate for what only he could give me, I kissed him back.

A growl ripped from his chest and he shoved his boxers down. Sucking my tongue into his mouth, he fisted himself and pushed inside me.

My shocked gasp only fed his dominance. His thumb stroked my clit and he sank to the hilt. With my legs spread wide, I grasped at his neck and arched into him. Tears dripped down my face and I let every single thing go except him.

His cock throbbed and my pussy pulsed. His tongue stroked and mine followed. His hands caressed and my nipples hardened. I dripped with a desire so overwhelming, I cried out for release.

Six feet four inches of solid muscle and seduction rode me hard. Huge hands wound into my hair and yanked. My head fell back and he rose up on his elbows. His body over mine, his lips a whisper of breath from mine, he thrust. His hips slammed into my clit and his hard length hit my G-spot.

Fire, light, heat, pain, I sucked in air through my teeth. Falling tendrils of pleasure licked up my body like a drug and I begged. "*Again.*"

Alex Vega didn't fuck me.

He consumed me.

Over and over, short thrusts pounded my body into submission. Every slam of his hips against my clit, every punishing stroke of his giant cock, he took me further. Desperate, not wanting this to ever end, I tried to hold on, but his body was a weapon and I never had a chance.

My muscles tensed, my feet curled and a thousand pounds of exquisite, painful release rushed me. I careened over the edge.

A roar ripped from his chest as he slammed home and his hot come pumped inside me.

Shaking, pulsing, I fought for air. Beads of sweat ran down my body as his seed dripped out of me. My eyes closed and my head fell back on the pillow, but I didn't get a single heartbeat to relax.

Hot mouth and biting teeth closed over my nipple.

"*Ahhh!*" My back flew off the bed as my pussy clenched around his still buried cock. I dug my hands into his biceps as he bit my other nipple. I didn't even have time to ask him what he was doing.

His cock still hard and deep inside me, he sat up, threw one of my legs over and flipped me to my stomach. Grabbing my hips, he brought me up on my knees and thrust so deep I felt him in my soul.

"Fuck, I love feeling my come in your tight cunt."

"Alex." Panting, spent, I wanted to say stop, but my quivering pussy and shaking thighs wanted more. "I can't." *Oh my God.* "Please."

"Yes you can." He pulled out but shoved two fingers in deep and rotated. "You're going to come again, sweetness. Just like this." His cock thrust back into me and a wet finger teased my ass. "On your knees, taking me so deep you forget everything except my name."

I didn't tell him I was already there. I was pushing back on his cock and surrendering every last one of my broken pieces as four letters bled from my lips and I begged for more. "*Alex.*"

His finger slipped inside my ass.

Exquisite pressure made me moan. "Yes, *more.*"

"You greedy little vixen." He slapped my ass.

My muscles clamped down on him from the shock of the sting.

His voice turned to gravel. "You're so fucking wet for me. I feel you pulsing. But you're not gonna come yet." His chest covered my back and he licked up my neck and bit my ear. "Oh no, sweetness." He pulled almost all the way out and I whimpered. "You're gonna let it build." His heat abruptly left my back and he slapped the other side of my ass.

I groaned.

"That's it." The head of his cock rubbed over my clit once, then he pulled away.

I almost came. "Please!"

Another slap. "Please what, sweetness? I can't hear you." His finger drew slowly in and out of my ass.

I lost it. "Fuck me!"

He slammed into me so hard we both groaned.

Then he fucked me.

Rhythmic and hard and raw, he *fucked* me. He pinched my clit, sank his thumb into my ass and pounded my pussy so hard he bottomed out on every thrust. My nipples turned painfully hard and a split second before I came, every muscle in my body jerked.

Stars exploded behind my eyes.

My thighs shook, my head fell back and the most intense orgasm I'd ever had stole my breath. My arms gave out, I hit the bed and he followed suit. His chest covered my back and with one last thrust, he stilled then pulsed deep inside me.

His huge hand gripped my jaw and turned my head. "Do you feel my come inside you?" His voice, low and dominant, covered my insecurities with his commanding presence.

"Yes," I breathed.

"You're more than in my arms."

SEVENTEEN

Alex

SHE FUCKING OWNED ME.

EIGHTEEN

Olivia

MY HEART SLAMMED AGAINST MY CHEST AND MY stomach fluttered.

You're more than in my arms.

He licked across my bottom lip and sank his tongue into my mouth then he pulled back just enough to speak against my lips. "Every time you stand tonight…." He thrust his hips against mine and his release slid between my walls and his cock. "I wanna see my come dripping down those sexy legs."

You're more than in my arms.

I'd been closed off for so long, I wanted to fight against every word that came out of his mouth and every slow grind of his body against mine. But my heart was grasping at his dominant arrogance and my pussy was pulsing around him as if I hadn't just come. "No." The single syllable was the only thing I dared to let come out because all I kept hearing was his voice….

You're more than in my arms.

"Yes," he growled as he slowly pulled out. "No shower, no underwear, you're going to smell and feel me all over you tonight. Know why?"

That shouldn't have been sexy but it was. So, so sexy

and I was ready for him to come inside me again, just to feel more of him. "No."

His rough hands gripped my waist and turned me over. His eyes searched my face, and for a single heartbeat, time stopped. "Because this?" He cupped me. "Is mine."

My whole world slanted.

Breath against breath, skin against skin, hope against despair, everything that was missing in my life, it broke through my defenses and filled my heart as his lips sweetly touched my forehead.

Then just as quickly, it was gone.

An impenetrable mask slid over Alex's expression and he shut everything down. Abruptly releasing me, he got out of bed. "Come on, we're going to eat."

His seductive dominance gone, his bossy attitude slid into place like a shield. I struggled to keep my face and voice even. "I'm not hungry." As if on cue, my stomach growled.

His mouth quirked in a maddeningly sexy way as he pulled on his tight-fitting boxers. "Yes you are."

I rolled over and buried my face in a pillow that now smelled like him. "I'm not going anywhere." Not with him. I couldn't. I needed to lie right here and tell myself he was bad for me until I believed it, but every second more in his presence, I was losing all the reasons I shouldn't be around him.

A thick finger expertly slipped into my pussy and destroyed my train of thought.

I gasped and involuntarily arched my ass up as he pressed down on my front walls. "What are you doing?"

He stroked side to side. "You're getting up or I'm gonna put you through a workout that'll leave you sore for a week."

I groaned, wondering if I could seriously come again as he worked me like a pro.

His breath touched the back of my neck. "Before you consider it, know this." He slipped a second digit inside me, spread his fingers wide and made short little thrusts in and out as he dropped his voice. "I'm going to make you work for it." Slow and twisting, he pulled his fingers out.

I whimpered. "I hate you."

"No, you don't." His teeth grazed my ear then his heat left my back. "Get up before I spank that luscious ass into an orgasm."

Hangers rattled in my closet as if he were searching through my clothes, and I crawled off the bed only because I was afraid he wasn't kidding. I'd planned on locking myself in the bathroom until he left, but the second I was vertical, he handed me a scrap of clothing.

"Wear this."

I glanced up and was struck all over again by how utterly beautiful he was. Every feature was locked into a seriousness so intense, I wondered if all of his smiles had been an act.

Swallowing the thought down, I remembered my mission. "I'm going to shower."

"No you're not." He took the material from my hands and slipped it over my head.

A dress I'd bought on impulse years ago stretched over my curves. It was tight, black, and had a plunging neckline. I'd gotten the stupid thing in hopes of wearing it for Jesse sometime. But that sometime never materialized and I'd forgotten about it. Until now.

Skimming my thighs with the backs of his hands, Alex pulled the dress down to where it landed just above my knees. "Sexy, sweetness." He stood back and took in every inch of my body as a slow smile spread across his face. "*Very sexy.*"

Remnants of what we'd just been doing dripped between my legs and my face flushed. "I'm not going out like this."

He buttoned his dress shirt. "Like what?"

I glanced down at my breasts, which were practically hanging out of the deep V, and then at my thighs, wondering how far the drip had gotten. "I'm a mess and I need a bra." Tendrils of tingling awareness raced across my skin as another drip of his orgasm fell down my thigh. God help me, I wanted to reach between my legs and feel just how much I'd made him come. "And underwear." I needed underwear—immediately—because if I didn't stop those drips and the constant arousal they were causing, I was going to go   mad.

He finished buttoning his shirt and stepped up to me. His hands cupped my face and his smile disappeared. He studied me so intently, I thought he would kiss me. I *wanted* him to kiss me. Without thinking, I pulled my bottom lip into my mouth, released it, then leaned forward.

His nostrils flared then he abruptly stepped back. "You're going just like that." The side of his mouth tipped up but it felt practiced. "The just-fucked look suits you."

Fucked.

One single word and reality slammed back home. I wasn't more than in his arms. I was standing three feet away but the distance he'd just put between us may as well have been a mile. Irrational hurt surged and I silently cursed myself. This was why I needed to back off. It didn't matter what he'd said before, there wasn't anything between us except fucking. Every move he made was practiced. I knew a player when I saw one. And that's exactly what he was—a player and a casual screw with a penchant for bossiness.

Just because I'd told him about my brother didn't make him my boyfriend, or even a friend for that matter. He was a stranger. A stranger I'd let come inside me. Inhaling, I unconsciously rubbed my thighs together, because despite my brain telling me to back the hell off, my pussy was aching so bad for his touch it was pulsing. "I need the bathroom." I didn't wait for his approval, I retreated.

Except he followed.

When the door didn't close behind me, I glanced up and caught our reflection in the mirror. My eyes wide on my face, my hair a mess, I watched as his features morphed into aggressive determination.

His gaze on mine, he yanked a towel off the rank and caged me in at the counter. Taller and wider than me, more muscles than a Greek god, he stood behind me and frowned.

"What's wrong, sweetness, you don't like me inside you?" Except he didn't say *sweetness* like he usually did. It wasn't playful or practiced, it was tinged with anger.

Surprised by his sudden change in demeanor, I didn't give him attitude. "I'm dripping."

"And?" he bit out.

Thrown, I didn't dare take my eyes off his in the mirror. "It's running down my leg."

The towel still in one hand, he pulled my dress up to my waist. We both followed his movement in the mirror then my gaze dropped to my pussy. It glistened with his come and my desire.

"Touch yourself," he demanded.

Shocked, turned on and completely off-balance, my voice wavered. "No."

"*Now.*"

My hand automatically went between my legs.

His eyes darkened.

My fingers fluttered across my wet heat. "Like this?" I whispered, suddenly desperate for his approval.

"Harder." His jaw clenched.

I dragged a finger across my opening and over my clit. The pressure made me ache a thousand times worse for his touch. "Help me," I begged.

His free hand gripped a handful of my hair and he tilted my head. My neck exposed, he put his mouth against my skin and his breath slid across me like a jolt of fire. My pussy throbbed, I sank my middle finger inside myself, and he thrust his hips against my ass. "I said *harder.*"

My palm hit my clit, I ground down on myself, and he drew his hips back. "No," I cried, needing that pressure, needing him.

The sound of his zipper and clank of a buckle filled my bathroom as he bit my ear. "Arch," he commanded.

I didn't need any more instruction. I grabbed the edge of the counter and thrust my ass toward him. He plunged to the hilt and the zipper on his pants dragged against my pussy. An incoherent sound crawled up my chest and spilled out of my mouth as he stretched my very sensitive, very sore, very used flesh. "*Arrhhh.*" Nothing had ever felt better.

Alex groaned, but then his thrust turned gentle. "You get tighter every time I'm inside you."

My fingers gripped the counter, but he grabbed one of my hands and placed it back on my clit.

"Stroke." He wrapped an arm around my waist for support and spoke hoarsely against my neck. "Make yourself come."

Only a few inches in either direction, he moved in and out of me. My body already conditioned by his, I stroked myself. His hold on me firm, his scent all around me, his dominance in every calculated move, it didn't take long. My legs started to give, my hand moved erratically across my flesh, and I started to come.

Pulling back then slamming into me, he growled. "Feel that?" He thrust three more times. "I'm gonna come inside you again."

"Yes." Oh my God, how was I talking? "*Please.*" I needed to feel him come before I did.

"Know why?" he asked as he thrust deep and ground his hips.

My thighs shook and desire crawled up my spine as everything he could do to my body culminated in this one moment and demanded release. "Why?" I whimpered, not even knowing what I was asking.

"Because this pussy is mine."

He came inside me and I fucking fell apart.

NINETEEN

Alex

I WAS LOSING MY GODDAMN MIND.

She had me going off like a fucking hair trigger. Cocked and loaded, one thrust inside her and she set me off.

Coming inside her had me higher than unloading hundreds of rounds at insurgents downrange. I'd held her tight and pumped more come into her in the past hour than I'd ever come in my fucking life. Two seconds after I felt her tight heat fill up with my seed, I was ready to fuck her again.

I knew she was sore. I felt her swollen walls constrict around me and regret punched my chest as she trembled while I pulled out. "Easy." I was a fucking asshole for taking her again.

"I'm good."

Her voice was so weak, I should've put her back to bed, but I was too selfish.

I ran hot water over the towel still in my hand and held it between her legs. "You're more than good, gorgeous." She wasn't just gorgeous, she was so fucking beautiful she had me punch-drunk just looking at her.

Her head fell back against my chest and her eyes closed. "You said no cleaning up."

"I know what I said." And I meant it. The second she'd made for the shower, I went fucking caveman. Shit brewed in my head and irrational anger surged at the thought of her wanting to erase my mark off her body. "This is all you get." I wiped once then threw the towel down. "You need a minute for your hair or makeup?"

"No."

My eyes narrowed. "Why?"

"Because I'm not going anywhere."

Leaning all her weight on me, well and truly fucked, she had no idea how much I was getting off seeing her like this. "Yes you are. You, me, food. Put your hair up." I didn't want other men looking at that thick mane that was mine to pull and mine to wrap my hands in. "You have three minutes." I was starving.

Sultry blue eyes popped open and a trace of the defiance that made me fucking hard sparked in her expression. "Screw you."

I smiled. "Anytime, sweetness. Any fucking time." I stood her upright. "Two and half minutes." She had as long as it took me to call the restaurant.

"Or what?" she taunted.

Goddamn she was a handful. I grinned when I should've been forming an exit plan. "Or," I drew the word out like a threat and scanned the length of her sexy-as-hell curves. "I'll make you wish you didn't throw attitude at me." Fuck, even the thought made me hard.

"You're an animal."

"Only around you."

"Liar," she accused.

"Two minutes." I should've wished it was a lie, but I was

already in too deep to give a fuck. "You want to waste more time arguing with me?" She could give me shit all day. I fucking got off on it.

She picked up a brush. "There's something wrong with you."

No fucking shit. "Lucky for you." I winked and pulled my phone out to call the restaurant.

I couldn't take my eyes off her. I watched her as I told the hostess to change our reservation time. Her small hands put her hair up in a messy twist and she applied eyeliner with a gracefulness not many women had. Her movements were sexy as hell but she had no idea how beautiful she was.

When I hung up, she was looking at me in the mirror. "Does everybody just do what you want?"

I took my time checking out her curvy ass. "You worried you got competition?" I was asking for trouble with the question but she hadn't reacted when I'd said she was mine.

She rolled her eyes. "Do I look stupid?"

No, she didn't. She was smart and beautiful, and when she'd told me about her brother, I knew how fucking resilient she was. She had my respect for that alone. But add in what she wanted to do for all those veterans who came home so fucked they couldn't be alone in their own heads and I didn't just respect her, I admired the hell out of her.

Holding her gaze in the mirror, I stepped behind her. "Not what I asked."

She set down the tube of shit she'd been swiping across her eyelashes. "Seriously?"

I didn't like the tone of her voice. "Answer the question," I demanded.

Her hands went to her hips. "I may be the flavor of the

night, weekend, whatever, but that's all I am to you." She steeled her expression. "And vice versa."

Bull-fucking-shit. "You got a problem with short-term memory?" I'd told her she was mine, goddamn it. I'd never said that to a woman.

"My memory is fine." She yanked a drawer open and threw her brush in.

I spun her around. I knew who I was, I knew what I did, and I'd work that shit out somehow. But I'd meant every fucking word that'd come out of my mouth. "What did I say last night before I came inside you?"

Her attitude faltered and her cheeks pinked. "Every guy talks shit when he's trying to get laid."

"I'd already gotten laid." I grasped her chin. "*What* did I say?"

She averted her eyes.

Goddamn it. "Were you too drunk to remember?"

She shook her head.

"Look at me, Olivia."

Her clear blue gaze, wiped clean of attitude, looked up at me with gut-wrenching vulnerability. "I remember."

"Then tell me."

"You said you'd never... gone bareback."

I held her gaze. "Never."

She sucked in a breath. "That doesn't mean—"

"I don't share." Not her. No fucking way.

She pulled her chin out of my grasp. "Alex."

I cupped her and let her know exactly what I meant. "This is mine."

"Just because you declare something doesn't make it so."

"You seeing someone else?" I should've known then and

there exactly how fucked I really was, because just the thought of another prick touching her, ever, was making me fucking postal.

She sighed. "Do you really think I would've let you fuck me if I was?"

Hearing her say *fuck* was hot as hell. She looked like a sexy prude coed. So when that mouth of hers kicked in…. I shook my head and rubbed my thumb over her luscious bottom lip. "You've got a mouth on you, sweetness."

"I'm not sweet."

Yes, she was. In every sense of the word. "Would you prefer sexy as fuck?"

She didn't move out of my grasp but she pretended to be bored. "Do you ever turn it off?"

I wasn't sure which way she was going with that but it didn't matter. The answer was the same. "No. Put on heels, we're gonna be late."

"For the record, your bossy attitude isn't going to get you anywhere with me."

Oh, yes it was. The more commanding I was, the more she responded, and I loved every fucking second of it. I leaned down to her ear and she melted into me. "I want you in sexy high heels." I ran a finger down her neck, between her breasts and skimmed the swell of her hip. "Just so we're clear…." I dragged my hand up her thigh and through her wet heat. "*This* is all mine. Until I say so, there's no one else for you."

She laughed but there was a nervous edge to it. "And you, *Mr. Cougar*, are going to be monogamous?"

I stiffened at the dig and for the first time in three years, my clients felt like more than a job, they felt like a fucking noose. I pressed my thumb into her clit. "I'm only going to be coming inside this pussy, sweetness." It wasn't a lie.

She grabbed my arms and her eyes closed for a second. The look of pure desire on her face made my dick throb, and because I had no self-control around her, I sank my finger inside her.

Her grip dug into my biceps and she sucked in a sexy little breath. Angel-blue eyes fluttered open and she looked hazily up at me. "You don't even know me."

She had no clue. No fucking *clue*. But she was about to because I decided then and there I wasn't going to fuck with this girl. Not when I could help it. I slowly pulled my finger out of her tight heat. "Three years."

She licked her bottom lip. "What?"

I couldn't stop myself. I grasped her face and sank my tongue into her mouth. Two strokes and I pulled back just enough to speak. "I left the Marines three years ago and nothing since has held my attention." I touched my lips to hers. "Until you."

Killing changed a man, but I didn't say that shit. She didn't need to know that surviving a firefight was a high I'd spent a whole damn year after the Marines trying to replicate. Fucking was a distant third, fucking for money only slightly better, but until the very moment I'd sunk inside her, I hadn't found shit that actually compared. Sure, I'd been fueled by money and fucking. I got off on making bank and bending women to my will, but being inside her? Being with her? It was so fucking different, I couldn't categorize it. I didn't want to. I just wanted more.

She stilled but her hands tightened on my arms.

I laid it out. "I see the look in your eyes when I'm inside you. I know how your body responds to mine. I heard every word when you told me about your brother. You're not casual, Olivia Toussaint, and I'm not fucking with you."

"Alex," she whispered.

I didn't give her a chance to respond. "We both want what's happening here, but I want more." I held her gaze so she knew just how serious I was. Then I did something that just about fucking killed me. "Put your shoes on and come to dinner with me, or walk away right now." I stepped back.

"But I don't—"

"Decide."

Her chest rose and fell twice. "I don't know you."

I dropped the mask I kept firmly in place and stared at her.

She crossed her arms protectively in front of herself. "You're asking a lot."

I didn't comment. I stared. This was the one and only time she was going to see me like this because I didn't beg. Ever.

Her head fell back and she sighed. "I don't know who's crazier, you or me." She glanced at me before going to her closet. "And I'm not wearing high heels because you told me to." She stepped into a sexy pair of sandals that made her five inches taller. "These just happen to go with the dress."

My heart pounding like I'd been sprinting with a full combat loadout, I didn't smile. "Ready?"

"My hair is a mess, you're making me wear a skintight dress with no underwear, and I have a sleeping pill hangover. Do I look ready?"

She looked exactly like I wanted her to look—fucked and taken. "Yes."

"You're a perv."

I was already thinking about making her come in the restaurant. "You have no idea."

TWENTY

Olivia

IT WAS OFFICIAL. I WAS OUT OF MY EVER-LOVING MIND.

I shoved my feet in shoes I'd regret in three seconds and pretended he wasn't dripping out of me as I sauntered to the front door. Full of bravado that was in direct contrast to nausea that was about to make me dry heave my insecurities all over the front hallway, I threw out some attitude because it was all I had left. "This better be a spectacular restaurant."

The side of his mouth tipped up, but if I didn't know any better, I'd say he looked almost shell-shocked. Then again, the set to his jaw could just be a reflection of his bossy-as-hell temperament. How would I even know? I knew *nothing* about him except that he was hung like a legend and fucked like a rock star.

And I'd just agreed to what? Dinner and a lifetime of submissive sex?

Oh my God.

I was out of my damn mind.

He ushered me out of my apartment and pulled the door shut behind us. "Pietra's."

The second I heard the name, I froze on the top step. "I'm not going there commando." The most expensive restaurant in Miami and not only did he have reservations that supposedly took six months to get, but he'd just called and demanded they change our reservation time? *And I was going there without underwear?*

His huge hands wrapped around my waist as his breath touched my ear. "Yes you are."

I shivered but then I let him guide me downstairs because I seemed to lose all my brain cells every time he went bossy on me.

His suit cut perfectly, his hair not looking at all disheveled, he guided me to his ridiculously expensive car with a hand at my back. Every move he made was either so practiced that he didn't have to think about it or he was the most confident man I'd ever met. Either way, just watching him open a car door was enough to make me wet. And that brought out my attitude.

I smiled sweetly at him and hiked the hem of my dress up to almost indecent. "I'm going to make a mess all over your pretty leather seats." I slid into the passenger seat, stupidly thinking I'd won a round, but he squatted at the open door.

His huge hand caught my chin and jaw as the side of his mouth tipped toward pure trouble. "Do you know what happens to sexy little vixens who test me?"

I pressed my thighs together and amped up my sugary smile. "What happened to sweetness?"

"I push back, *sweetness.*" In one graceful move, he stood to his full height and quietly lowered the door.

The spicy scent of him and new leather surrounded me and I knew—I was so out of my league.

He got behind the wheel and pulled into traffic like he

was born to drive. I leaned my head back against the seat and sighed.

He picked up my hand as if he were my boyfriend. "Tired?"

"I kinda hate you."

His laugh was unexpected. Deep and rich, it sounded too much like a life I wanted.

He brought my hand to his lips and brushed a kiss across my knuckles. "Why's that?"

"You're too perfect." He drove like he fucked and like he did everything else—with skill.

He released my hand but it was too casual to tell if it was on purpose. "What are you insecure about, sweetness?"

I glanced at his profile in the passing streetlights. It was as perfect as everything else about him. "You do that a lot, answer a question with a question."

"You're avoiding answering me."

Maybe it was because his car was like a cocoon to the outside world, maybe it was because nothing in the past twenty-four hours felt real, but I answered him honestly. "I'm not insecure. I haven't had time to be. I've spent the past two years working my ass off to get my charity off the ground and still pay rent on my shit apartment. When I'm not dead tired, I think about my brother. And occasionally I used to wonder why Jesse didn't want me like I wanted him. But now?" Being with Alex? "I don't give a shit." And if I was being honest with myself, which I wasn't, I'd acknowledge I was pissed at Jesse.

Alex was quiet a moment, and I thought he'd ask why I didn't give a shit, but instead he zeroed in on something I didn't want to talk about.

"Why don't you have a dog?"

The practiced response rolled off my tongue. "I can't have pets at my place."

He looked sideways at me. "You're lying."

I shifted my bare thighs against the soft leather and regretted hiking up my dress. "Ask my landlord if you don't believe me."

"Not what I meant. There're plenty of places you could've rented that'd allow it."

I stared out the window at the colorful lights of South Beach. I didn't know how Alex picked up on it, but he was right. I wanted a dog. I wanted a lot of dogs. I'd take home every one at the shelter if I could. But my brother couldn't have a dog and he'd wanted one. He'd asked me to go to the humane society with him before he'd died and I'd asked why. I'd stupidly, selfishly, ignorantly *asked why*.

A warm hand wrapped around my nape. "Hey."

I flinched and realized belatedly that we'd pulled up in front of the restaurant. "What?"

He released my neck, grasped my chin and turned me to face him. For three heartbeats, he searched my face. Then he nodded once. "You can tell me what just happened after you eat." He kissed me. No tongue, no innuendo, just the brush of his lips against mine.

My vulnerable heart grasped at the gesture and dangerously put more stock in it than anything else in the past two years.

I was still trying to shove all my emotions down when Alex beat the valet to my door and opened it. As discreetly as I could, I pulled the hem of my dress down, and like a gentleman, Alex helped me out of the car. But the second I was vertical, he released his hold on me to shake hands with the valet.

I didn't know if it was the sex or the sleeping pill or not

having eaten, but the sudden loss of contact destroyed my equilibrium and a wave of dizziness made me stumble.

"Olivia." The quiet sternness to his voice belied the force with which his hand hit the small of my back.

Except he didn't pull me into an embrace. His arm didn't go around my shoulders. He didn't grasp at my arms to steady me. His hand took up all the real estate on my lower back and he stepped against the side of my body like a shield. Pushing me into him, using his strength to brace me, he looked down and barked out a question that demanded an answer. "You going to faint?"

The air cracked and humidity pressed against my skin as if there was a sudden change in barometric pressure.

"*Olivia.*"

Wind swirled around us and tossed strands of my hair into my face. "I'm okay."

His hand brushed across my face and tucked my hair into place. "When was the last time you ate?"

Everything he did was practiced. "I don't know." Why was he so good at this? Wind kicked the palms into a clatter then lightning flashed across the sky. A low rumble of thunder built to a nerve-jumping growl and I shivered.

His gaze fixed on me, Alex didn't even glance at the sky. "Inside. Now."

The hostess nodded discreetly at Alex and led us immediately to a table.

My stomach growled and thunder rattled the front windows. Conversations didn't even pause in the full restaurant. Silverware clanked, people laughed, waiters hustled through a busy dinner rush, but no one looked at the ominous sky or knew that my brother was dead.

A studious-looking waiter met us at our table as the hostess seated us. "Good evening, Mr. Vega. Ma'am." He opened my menu and handed it to me. "Thank you for braving the storm to join us tonight. Would you care for wine?"

Alex rattled off a Scotch order for himself and white wine for me.

The waiter retreated with a nod.

Lightning lit up the space and I glanced around a restaurant I'd never be able to afford on my hourly wages.

Alex didn't open his menu. "Why didn't you eat today?"

"I did eat." I must have.

His measured stare was more charged than the brewing storm.

The waiter showed back up. He placed wine in front of me and Scotch and a glass of ice in front of Alex. "I'll give you a moment to look over the menu. Please let me know if you have any questions."

Alex dismissed him with a nod and picked up the glass of ice. "Pull your dress up." He poured the ice into his napkin.

Alarm spread across my skin like a cold chill. "What?"

"Spread your legs." He twisted the napkin.

I nervously glanced at the surrounding tables. Our backs were against a wall and the tablecloth more than covered my legs, but holy hell. "I'm not—"

He grasped my thigh, spread my legs, and put the ice between them.

I sucked in a breath as the cold hit my sore body.

His hand still generating heat on my leg, Alex pushed the ice against my entrance. "You're hungry, you're tired and you're sore. I'm going to feed you then I'm taking you to my place and putting you to bed."

Emotion lodged in my throat.

"Before you fall asleep, you're going to tell me what happened in the car." He squeezed my thigh, released me, then picked up the menu. "What do you like to eat?"

I blinked then the answer fell out of my mouth because I didn't know what to do with someone taking care of me. "Anything except red meat."

"Vegetarian?"

"No, I just don't eat red meat."

He nodded and closed the menu. "How long?"

"What?" My nerves shot, I didn't know how to act around him.

"How long have you not eaten red meat?" he asked patiently.

"Awhile." I was eight. My brother told me beef was really dog meat because Mom couldn't afford a cow.

He studied me. "What's going on?"

I pushed the thought of my brother away and dropped my gaze to my lap, barely refraining from pressing the ice against myself. Once the shock of the coldness had worn off, it felt good, really good. "How did you know, about the ice?"

He slid closer to me and cupped my face. This time, when his mouth touched mine, his tongue ran across my bottom lip, as if he were asking permission.

My heart, my body, they responded. I melted against him and let him kiss me.

Slow and languid, he possessed my mouth with no less dominance than his heated intrusion last night. He expertly teased my tongue to meet his then he swept through my mouth as if he knew every way to make me his. The second he had my pussy pulsing against the ice between my legs, he pulled back. "Stop being nervous."

My lips tingling, my skin feverish from his touch, I wasn't nervous. I was falling so hard I was terrified. Desperate, I glanced around the restaurant and grasped for a subject change. "I've never been here."

He winked. "The food is spectacular."

I ignored his teasing of my earlier statement because threads of jealously twisted in my gut. "Do you come here a lot?" I hated myself for even thinking it but it was impossible not to recognize that this was a date restaurant.

The waiter approached but Alex didn't take his eyes off mine. "We need a few minutes."

I picked up the menu.

"Olivia."

My eyes closed, and for one second, I breathed in the way he said my name. It wasn't a request or a question. It was dominating and commanding and nothing made me feel more like a woman.

And I needed to ignore it. "What's good?"

"Put the menu down."

"I'm in the mood for pasta." There weren't even prices listed. I guess if you had to ask, you couldn't afford to eat here.

The menu was plucked from my hands and his stare cut through my defenses. "I've never brought a woman here. I don't date."

The tidal surge of relief was undercut by reality. "Except when you escort older women to fundraisers."

His jaw ticked. "One-off."

I picked up my glass and swirled the pale wine. "Pretty sure lying to someone constitutes fucking with them." I took a sip. Ice cold and tart and perfect.

He waited until I set my glass down. "I don't *date*."

I got it. He fucked. Probably a lot. "But here we are."

His hand landed on the back of my neck, he leaned forward and his voice dropped. "I'm not going to date you, Olivia Toussaint." His blue-eyed gaze pierced me with warning. "I'm going to own you."

TWENTY-ONE

Alex

EVERY FUCKING INCH. I WAS GOING TO DOMINATE that tight pussy, lick those lush tits and taste every single curve on her body. I owned her. Because she owned me.

"How do you know my last name?" Breathy, nervous, her voice was still sexy as hell.

"Your phone."

She nodded.

"Hey, Sarge."

I looked up.

Mother. Fucking. *Fuck.*

I was going to kill him. "Jared," I bit out his name and tipped my chin as I glared at him. My hand still possessively on Olivia, I refused to look at two of my clients draped on either side of him. "What are you doing here?"

His lazy grin spread wide. "A little dinner." He checked out Olivia. "A little fun."

My shy client spoke. "You were in the military?"

Half of Jared's smile dropped. "Staff Sergeant Alexander Vega, Second Light Armored Reconnaissance Battalion, United States Marine Corp. You're looking at a real live hero,

162

ladies. He saved my life." He ground the last sentence out with zero gratitude.

My 10:00 p.m. cougar client dropped her gaze to my lap. "Oh, he's a hero all right." She licked her lips. "Too bad he's not working tonight." Her hand rubbed down Jared's chest. "He's missing all the fun."

Shit bottomed out in my stomach and I glanced at Olivia.

Her face ashen, she pushed away from me. "Excuse me." She stood.

Fuck. "Olivia." I reached for her but she was already walking away.

Glaring at Jared, I fished a few bills out of my wallet and threw them on the table. "We'll talk tomorrow."

"Sure." His grin returned. "But not too early." He kissed my shy client on the cheek then nipped my cougar client under the ear. "One way or another, I have a feeling it's gonna be a long night." He chuckled.

I didn't give two fucks about his threesome. He was an idiot for taking it out of the bedroom and every complication he'd just brought down on himself, but that was his fucking problem. I was too busy being enraged he'd paraded that shit in front of Olivia, knowing I would be here.

I strode outside and glanced up and down the street but she was gone. "Which way did she go?" I barked at the valet.

He pointed south. "She took the first left."

I jogged around the corner as lightning lit up the sky like a fucking omen but I found her. Her shoulders proud, her long legs moving at a fast clip, I took in the sight of her like a starved man and relief hit my chest. I didn't think. I went after her.

"What are you doing?" Sharp, accusing, pissed at Jared, pissed at myself, I didn't rein in my tone.

"Fuck off." Her voice caught.

"*Stop*," I commanded.

She picked up her pace. "I'm not going to be anyone's fool, especially not yours."

Completely out of my mind, I grabbed her and pushed her against the side of the building and my mouth descended over hers.

Her gasp swallowed by my dominance, she didn't push back.

I devoured her. Hands gripping, tongue searching, I stroked through her mouth with a desperation I'd never experienced before. I forced a leg between hers, leaned my body into hers and frantically, single-mindedly kissed her.

I wanted to erase the past three years and forget about the scene in the restaurant. I wanted to undo the bullshit I'd caused at her fundraiser and I wanted to be anything except what I was.

But she didn't kiss me back. Her body didn't melt into mine. Her arms didn't come around my neck. No sounds came from her throat. And I was who I was.

My chest tight, I pulled back as I gripped her nape. I was unraveling and she was the thread. I knew what was coming but my only choice was to take it head on. "Talk to me."

So raw, it was almost without emotion, she spoke. "What do you do for work?"

Investments. It was on the tip of my tongue. The lie was so practiced, I'd almost convinced myself. Three years of this life. Guys envied me. Women wanted me. I was drowning in cash and pussy. I didn't need a goddamn thing—until twenty-four hours ago. Now I was staring at the one thing I wanted more than walking out of the Marines with both legs attached, and I didn't speak. I couldn't.

"She…." Her chest rose with an inhale. "She said you weren't working tonight."

Air somehow managed to move in and out of my lungs. "I'm not."

"But you work nights."

I stared into her gorgeous eyes. I could lie, tell her I stripped, bartended, hell, tell her the truth and say I used to fuck for money. I had investments, I had money. I didn't need my clients anymore. I didn't even want them. I could walk away from that life right fucking now. But I didn't say any of that. Because stupidly, idiotically, I thought we had something special and I wanted more. I wanted her without having to lie. "I'm an escort."

Her throat moved with a swallow and her voice dropped to a whisper. "What kind of an escort?"

My heart pounded. My mouth went dry. "Women pay me for sex."

She jerked back.

I let go of her. But the memory of every single moment of being inside her felt like it was ripped out of my grasp. "Olivia."

One hand flew up and she started shaking her head.

I opened my fucking mouth. "Every word I said, I meant. This isn't casual—"

"*Casual*?" She hit my chest, hard. "You fucked me! *Without a condom.*"

The disgust in her voice, all over her face, it gutted me. Then the past three years swelled into defiance and pushed the wrong goddamn buttons. "I'm clean. I told you that. I'm not an irresponsible dick like the asshole who left you to walk home by yourself."

"*Oh my God.*" Tears dripped down her face. "You're comparing yourself to him? *You're the liar.* You sell yourself to anyone willing to pay for it and you think Jesse's an asshole? You're lying to yourself if you think that's not fucked-up!"

I may have withheld information, but fuck her. She didn't know what the fuck I did, or what I told myself. "I never lied."

She fucking lost it. "You should have told me! You don't go around fucking women without telling them you're a *prostitute.*" She spit the last word out like she was equating me to a murderer. "I should've had a choice." She pounded on her chest. "Me. *My choice.* But you didn't say shit. That's like an addict not warning someone they stick needles in their arm!"

My temper exploded. "You're calling me a goddamn junkie? You think I stick my dick in diseased women and fuck clients without protection? *What the fuck?*"

"Oh, OH. Clients? Is that what you call it? Nice justification. Like you're some high-priced lawyer who has *clients.*"

My laugh was bitter. "I make more an hour than any lawyer, sweetness, don't kid yourself."

"Ohmigod, I'm gonna be sick." She pivoted and started to walk away.

It only fueled my anger. "That's it," I taunted. "Walk away. It's the one thing you're good at."

She spun and let loose. "You don't know me. Not one single thing. You don't know what I'm good at or what I'm not. If you want to talk about walking away, look in the fucking mirror, you goddamn hypocrite. I didn't throw away intimacy just to waste it on some *client*. I'm not some sick kinky fuck who gets off on charging money for sex. So fuck you. You did this, not me. You fucked me knowing exactly who you were. You walked away before I even stepped foot in the game!"

She was dead on, but I hated her for being right. The moment I saw her in that penthouse, I knew she was different. I just didn't care. I wanted to get my dick wet in her and that's all I was focused on because I hadn't felt anything like that for years. "I'm not the one walking away from a fully funded charity."

"And I'm sure as hell not some idiot who thinks I'm so good at sucking dick that I can make a male prostitute go straight. So keep your fucking money. A PTSD service dog charity backed by a male escort is the last fucking thing I want to be a part of."

"Then don't partner with me. Take your fucking money and do something useful with it. And for the record, you never sucked my dick." This time, I turned and walked away from her. I was raging fucking mad, but if I stopped for half a second to think about it, I'd realize I was only pissed at myself.

Lightning flashing, thunder rolling, I stormed back to the valet. "The McLaren."

The valet jumped to attention. "Right away, sir. I put it in the garage because of the storm. It'll be just a minute, sir."

He ran down the street toward the garage and my cougar client stepped out of the restaurant sans Jared.

She glanced around. "Where's your girlfriend?"

"She's not my girlfriend." *Girlfriend*. What the fuck was I thinking?

"Ah, with the way she stormed out, I thought...." She trailed off.

I ignored her.

She stepped up beside me. "You passed me off to your young friend."

"He'll take care of you."

Her hand ran down my arm. "I like the way you take care of me."

She liked any man who *took care* of her. "I'm sure you'll survive." Where the fuck was the valet?

"Maybe you should take me home and work off some of the tension you're holding on to."

I was pissed enough to glance at her pussy then her tits. "Maybe I should."

She smiled. "Now you're speaking my language." Her hand hooked under my arm.

I stared her down. "But I'm not going to. Want to know why?" I didn't care about losing her as a client. I'd fucking had it.

She dropped the fake flirting pretense and my arm and sighed. Her voice lowered to its natural cadence and she shook her head. "Look, you want advice from a woman old enough to be your mother?"

"You're only forty, you're not old enough to be my mother, but go ahead." God knows, I never got shit for advice from my own mother.

"Go after her. Her face didn't drop like that because she didn't have feelings for you. A woman only looks that upset when she's in love." She shook her head and walked off. "Stupid girl."

The valet pulled up with my car.

TWENTY-TWO

Olivia

I VOMITED.

My stomach lurched and I heaved but there was nothing left.

I'd slept with him. I'd fucked a male prostitute—*without a condom*—and I'd fallen for him. Fallen for everything about him, even though I knew I shouldn't have trusted him. Oh my God, *I'd trusted him.*

Another round of nausea crawled up my throat as my phone vibrated in my purse and I dry heaved. Wedged behind a dumpster in an alley, I cursed my stupidity. Lightning lit up the sky and thunder followed like the universe was casting judgment.

Gagging at the smell of rotting food and urine and who the hell knew what else, I fished through my purse for a tissue. But what I really needed was a redo. I wanted to rewind the whole stupid weekend and undo every single decision I'd made. I didn't want to know what it felt like to have him inside me. I didn't want to hear his deep, commanding voice in my head. I didn't want to know what being taken by a man like that meant. I wanted my ignorance back. I wanted the walls of grief that'd protected me from throwing my heart out there back.

Tears dripped down my face and thunder boomed even closer.

I told myself it was a mistake, that it was just a setback. But the second I thought the words, my heart hurt. It didn't want that asshole to be a mistake. It wanted every way he'd held me to be real. A raindrop landed on my shoulder and I stumbled out of the alley just as a familiar sports car crept up.

"*Shit.*" Shit, shit, shit. My heart pounding, I jumped back as Alex cruised past.

Scanning the other side of the street, he didn't see me.

My phone buzzed again. Ignoring it, I waited until he turned the corner then I hustled as fast as I could in my stupid heels. Most every storefront was retail and I had to walk two blocks before I found a bar. As I stepped inside, the big raindrops that'd been taunting me gave way to a torrential downpour.

I went straight to the restroom and locked myself in a stall. Taking my cell out, I ignored the seven missed calls from Alex and dialed a cab company. They answered on the first ring.

"Hi, I need a cab at—"

The operator cut me off. "I'm sorry, ma'am, but we've pulled all our drivers back in."

Wait. "What?"

"The tropical storm was just upgraded to a hurricane. Stay safe, ma'am." He hung up.

A hurricane?

I pulled up Uber. An automated message popped up. *Due to hurricane-force winds, Uber services are temporarily suspended in your area....*

Thunder shook the building.

I pulled up my weather app.

How the hell had I missed this? A tropical storm had picked up speed and force and unexpectedly changed course at the last minute. A category two hurricane was heading straight for Miami and projected landfall was the middle of the night. *Tonight.*

Oh my God. The dogs.

I didn't have a choice. I called Jesse. Six rings and it went to voice mail.

"Hey, um, it's me. I know things are… shit. I know things suck between us right now, but I was wondering if I could get a ride to the kennel? I'm sorry to bug you, but cabs are already shut down and it's too late to take the bus and I'm worried about the dogs. So, um, yeah, you're probably busy, but you know, if you get this?" *Fuck.* I hung up and two seconds later he called back.

"Hey—"

Rain and wind howled in the background. "I'm busy right now, Liv. What do you need?"

Except he didn't sound like he really wanted to know what I needed. He sounded pissed as hell. "Um, never mind, you're busy. I get it." I started to hang up.

"*Liv*," he barked.

"No, it's okay, never mind." Thunder boomed again.

His voice softened marginally. "When I finish securing this building site, I'll come get you and take you back to my place. It's safer than yours." He paused. "Jennifer is already there."

Ah yeah, no thanks. Not a chance. I grew up in Florida. I wasn't afraid of waiting out a hurricane. "I'm going to the kennel. The dogs will be scared alone."

"You were fired."

I didn't need reminding. But I still had the keys and my boss had never stepped foot in that place, so she could go fuck herself for all I cared. She didn't care about the animals anyway. She'd never know I was there, and hanging out with the dogs would be a thousand times better than staring at Jennifer and Jesse in the dark. Fuck that. "I still have my keys and I'm going to check on them. I need to go." It was going to suck walking all that way but I needed to start now before the winds really picked up.

"You don't have a car."

"I'll figure it out."

He paused. "Give me two hours. I'll give you a ride."

I could be there by then. "Don't worry about it, just take care of Jennifer."

"Damn it, Liv. I'm not back together with her."

"Whatever." I hated that I was on the verge of tears. "It's your life."

He sighed like he did when he was really tired, and my heart hurt. "I'll ask Talon if he can give you a ride. Call you back in a second." He hung up before I could protest.

I stared at the skanky bathroom stall, mentally counting the blocks to my apartment and wondering why the hell I'd sold my car for a pipe dream.

Jesse called back in less than a minute. "Talon will be at your apartment in fifteen minutes."

"I'm not at home."

Pause. Then, "Please tell me you're not at his place."

"I'm at a bar."

The sigh was louder this time. "A hurricane's coming and you go to a bar?"

"I was thirsty." It sounded better than saying I didn't know about the storm because I was busy screwing a male prostitute.

"Just tell me where you are, Olivia." He said my name like I was a child.

I told him the name of the bar.

"I'll let Talon know. You need any supplies? I can stop by the kennel on my way home."

"No." I wasn't a complete failure at life. I had some candles… somewhere. "I'm good."

"All right, I'll talk to you later. Talon will be there in a few."

I didn't know why I never thought about it before, but I realized right then that Jesse was always rescuing me. I didn't ever help him hang pictures or give him rides or cook him meals. What did I do for him? I exhaled. "Thanks."

"What's wrong?"

I was a shitty person. "Nothing. Thanks for getting me a ride."

"Hey."

"What?" My phone buzzed with another incoming call but I ignored it.

The background noise on his end got quieter. "I still want you to come to Ocala with me."

This time, a tear did fall down my cheek. "We can't go back, Jesse." I wasn't that sixteen-year-old girl who believed in heroes anymore. And his kiss? As much as I wanted it to be, it wasn't like Alex's. I loved Jesse, I did, but I realized now that I wasn't in love with him.

"I'm not looking to go back, Liv. I want a future."

"And you deserve one." With someone better than me.

"Liv."

I swiped at my cheek. "I love you, Jesse, I always will, but Jen's a nice girl. You should give her a second chance. I'll talk to you later. I'm going to go wait out front for Talon." I hung up before he had a chance to say anything else because I was too raw to talk to him anymore. If it weren't for the dogs at the kennel, I'd probably be running away to Ocala with him and screwing up both of our lives.

I made my way to the front of the bar just as Talon sauntered in. Unlike Jesse, he was all show. They were both blond and tall and muscular, but where Jesse was the guy next door, Talon was the player your mother warned you about. And it reminded me of Alex. If you put a suit on Talon, he'd have the same exact swagger as Alex. Maybe more so.

Every woman in the place turned to look at Talon. His hair wet from the rain, he caught my eye and grinned.

"What's up, darlin'?" He leaned down and kissed my cheek like we were old friends then took my hand and held my arm out. "Daaaamn." He spun me around. "Shame to waste this dress on a hurricane, firefly."

"What better time to wear it?" I asked dryly.

His laugh made people around us smile. "Full of fire too. No wonder you had Vegas all worked up." He glanced around. "Where is he?" His smile didn't falter but the glint in his eye went from playful to suspicious in less than half a second.

"Firefly?"

"Bright and unattainable." He dropped the pretense and the smile. "Where's Vegas?"

There was a definite edge to him that felt like more than a military background. "No clue. I'm not his keeper."

Talon eyed me. "He leave you here?"

"What makes you think I'd go out with him?" I wasn't about to admit to anyone I'd slept with a male escort.

Slow and calculated, he nodded. "You found out."

"Found out what?"

"Don't play games with me, darlin'."

"You here to grill me or give me a ride? Because I need to get going."

He didn't budge. "I know where you need to go, but I asked you a question."

My hands went to my hips. "Actually, you didn't ask me a question. You made a statement."

He threw his head back and laughed. "Shit, darlin', come on." He took his jacket off and put it around my shoulders. "Let's get you out of here before I decide to liquor you up."

The scent of coconuts and beach and man surrounded me as I glanced up at his too-blond hair and tanned skin. "You surf."

"Yes, ma'am. Every chance I get."

"Then why do you live in Florida?" Wasn't California or Hawaii the place to be if you were a diehard surfer?

"Who said I live here?"

I frowned. "You don't?"

"Not in Miami. C'mon, rain was holdin' back as I pulled up. Let's get in the car before it lets loose again."

With his arm securely around me, Talon led us to a new black Dodge Challenger and opened the door for me. I got in and the scent of beach and coconuts multiplied by a thousand. He slid behind the wheel as a gust of rain practically swamped the car.

"I didn't know about the storm," I admitted.

"Most people didn't." He started the engine then ran his hands over his hair. "Dirty devil snuck up on Florida. Only good news is that it's supposed to pass quickly."

I watched palm trees sway drastically in the wind. "You think it will hit hard?"

"No tellin'. I reckon it'll do exactly as it pleases."

"Where are you from?" His accent wasn't quite Southern but it wasn't quite Texan either.

"Little bit of everywhere, darlin'. You?"

"Florida, born and raised. Texas?"

He nodded. "I've lived there."

"Ah, the source of the twang."

He pulled onto the empty road but glanced at me and grinned. "You don't like my twang, firefly?"

Talon was all charm but he didn't have dark silky hair or a deep blue gaze that took me in and left no room to breathe. I changed the subject. "How do you know Jesse?"

"Same way I know Vegas."

I nodded. "The Marines."

Something clouded his expression but then it was quickly gone. "Once a Marine, always a Marine."

"So you knew Jesse and Alex, but they didn't know each other?"

"Nope."

"But you served together."

"Yep."

I fought from sighing. "Are you being cagey on purpose?"

"Are you gonna tell me what you were doin' with Vegas? Besides the obvious?"

Heat flamed my cheeks. "What *obvious*?"

"Oh, darlin," he chuckled. "All that defensiveness? You just told me everythin' I wanted to know."

I crossed my arms. "I didn't *pay* him."

His expression turned serious. "Didn't think you did."

"Don't tell Jesse."

"I won't, darlin', but you gotta understand how men think. The second he saw Vegas gunnin' for you, he already knew 'bout it. You've got him so worked up, he couldn't wait two hours to get you away from him."

"I wasn't with Alex when I called Jesse. And what does it matter anyway? Jesse and I are just friends."

"That isn't how he sees it."

Fucking hell. "So he sent you to get me only because he thought I was with Alex?"

Talon smiled like this was funny as hell to him. "Yep."

"And you just happened to be sitting around waiting for something to do?"

"Oh," he chuckled. "I was busy." He glanced at my dress then back at me and winked. "But I thought you'd be more fun." He grinned. "I was right."

Oh my God. "Are you flirting with me?"

"Darlin', if you have to ask, then I'm doin' a shit job of it."

"Your job isn't to flirt with me."

"No, that's just the icin', firefly. By the way, the whole no underwear thing?" He dropped his gaze to my tits, then my lap. "Sexy, darlin'."

Oh my God, I hated Alex for making me wear this dress. And myself for agreeing to it. And Talon, because he was here and Alex wasn't. "Go ahead, rub it in."

Talon laughed. "Don't worry, firefly, I'm sure Vegas loved every minute of it."

"I'm sure he did." I turned toward the window and realized I'd never told Talon where I lived. "Do you know where you're going?"

"Gotcha covered." He drove too fast through the rain. "So what happened tonight?"

"Nothing," I lied.

"Fifty bucks says you didn't wind up at that bar on purpose."

I sighed. I must have had a fucked-up psychological condition, something about dumping my inner shit on strangers, because my mouth opened and out it came. "I was on a date with Alex."

Talon looked affronted. "He took you to that dump?"

"No, Pietra's. We had a… disagreement." To say the least. "I left."

"What'd you argue 'bout?"

"Some guy came in with two women. The women seemed to…." My traitorous voice cracked. "They knew Alex." Heart-crushing jealousy reared up, and I hated Alex all over again. "Let's just say they really knew him."

"You ever dated a man with a past?" Talon asked casually.

"What's that supposed to mean? I'm not a prude."

"Never said you were. But what's the difference between sleepin' with some frat prick who's been with a hundred different women and sleepin' with a man who keeps a dozen or so women happy on a regular basis?"

A dozen? *All the time*? Like, *weekly*? My heart crushed just thinking about it. And the fear that'd been bubbling since he'd told me what he did for a living became a full boil. "I'm sure it's a lot more than a dozen." How the hell would he ever be satisfied with one woman? He had the stamina of a damn warrior.

"You sure 'bout that? You talk to him?"

"I'm not talking to him." He'd lied to me.

"So, you're judgin' him. How many men have you slept with?"

"That's none of your business," I snapped.

"Me?" He ignored my attitude. "I lost count a long time ago. But every one left happy." He glanced at me and grinned. "Am I any different because I never got compensated?"

"Seriously?" Was I really having this conversation? "You're justifying prostitution?"

He shrugged. "Oldest profession in the business."

"And what business is that?" Soul sucking?

"The business of life, darlin'."

I kinda hated him.

TWENTY-THREE

Alex

I CIRCLED HER BLOCK TWICE BUT NO LIGHTS WERE ON IN her place. The wind was kicking up, rain was fucking dumping, and I knew cabs weren't running. Where the fuck was she?

I called Neil. That Bob the Builder fuck Olivia called a best friend said he'd built my condo, but he didn't fucking build it, Neil Christensen had. But maybe Bob worked for him.

Neil picked up on the first ring. "Ja."

I'd met Neil, who's ex-Danish Military Special Ops, in Afghanistan when our units had worked together to take down a terrorist cell. He was fucking brutal in combat, and lethally quiet under every other circumstance. If his presence didn't scare the fuck out of you, there was something wrong with you. But he'd been more than decent to me. He came to the States after his service and became a commercial contractor. He'd given me a steal on my penthouse and five other units in the building during preconstruction. I'd sat on them for a year, and when I'd sold the first one, I'd made one-point-two million. I'd already told him I wanted in on his next project.

"It's Alex. I need a favor."

"I do not do favors." Despite being in the States for years, his accent was still thick.

"Bullshit, you sold me six condos at cost. But this isn't that kind of favor. The blond jarhead you and Talon were talking to at the fundraiser, he work for you?"

Silence.

"Come on, I don't have a beef with him. I just need his number."

"I am not getting involved for a female."

Omniscient fuck. Leave it to him to know this was about Olivia. "I just want to ask him a question." And fucking punch him. "Is he your foreman or something? You must have his number."

"Project Manager. He built out your units. If you paid attention, you would already have his number."

Goddamn it. "Name?" I probably had his number in my contacts. Neil had given me a number to call with any issues during construction, but I'd never needed to use it.

"The female is too good for you." He hung up.

"*Fuck.*" I pounded on the steering wheel and dialed her again but this time I left a message. "I don't give a shit what you think about me right now. You're out in a goddamn hurricane. *Call me.*" I hung up and my cell rang. I didn't look at the caller ID. "Where are you?" I barked.

Talon laughed. "You miss me?"

I should've called him first. "I want the number of the jarhead you were talking to at the fundraiser."

"Fixer?"

Goddamn it. "You and your fucking nicknames. I don't give a shit what you call him. Give me his number."

"How 'bout I do one better?"

"I don't have time for this right now," I warned.

He chuckled. "If you don't have time for a hot brunette with a slammin' body—"

I pulled over. "You have Olivia?" How *the fuck* did that happen?

"Firefly's got a mouth on her."

The rage was instant. "If you fucking touched her, you're dead."

He howled with laughter. "Pretty sure she's not into surfers."

"Quit fucking with me," I growled. "Where is she?"

"A kennel in south Miami."

What the fuck? "There's a hurricane coming and you took her to goddamn kennel?"

"That's where she wanted to go."

"And you thought that was fucking safe?"

"She ain't mine, bro. Not gonna tell your woman what to do."

Fuck. "Give me the address." I didn't tell him she wasn't mine.

He rattled off an address that was twenty-five minutes away. "I told you this would come back to bite you."

Distracted by the pounding rain, I spun the car around. "What the hell are you talking about?"

"The women."

Fuck him. "Not all of us are born with a silver spoon in our mouths, *bro*."

His tone sharpened. "You think I came from money?"

It wasn't the first time I'd heard him pissed but it was the first time he'd ever said shit about his past. "What difference does it make? You have money. I didn't. So I fucking earned it." I didn't know why the hell I was justifying my shit to him, except a blue-eyed gaze slayed with hurt was stuck on fucking repeat in my head and it was killing me.

"Earn it another way."

"Did I ask you for advice, you fucking manwhore? At least I get paid for that shit."

He ignored me. "She's classy, Vegas." He chuckled. "Even if she doesn't wear underwear."

If I ever saw him checking her out, I was going to pound his fucking face in. "Fuck you, Talerco."

"I'm all good." He drew the word *all* out then hung up.

The McLaren hydroplaned, and I cursed myself for not running back home to get my SUV, but I was mission intent. Seventeen minutes later, I pulled up to a piece-of-shit old bunker-style concrete block building. Half the parking lot was already flooded and the old slat windows looked like they'd break in a strong wind, let alone a hurricane. That was if they didn't become death projectiles first.

I parked as close as I could and stood under what was left of the awning as I pounded on the glass front door. Lights were on in back but there wasn't a single other car in the lot.

"Olivia!" I pounded harder to be heard over the wind but there was no response.

Goddamn it.

I ran back to the car and hit the horn several times until a light came on in the front. I rushed back under the awning and she came toward the door with two small dogs trailing her.

I took my first full breath since she'd walked out of the restaurant.

She stopped a foot short and crossed her arms. "What do you want?"

Was she fucking serious? "Open the goddamn door."

"I don't open doors for liars." Her voice muffled, she glanced down as one of the dogs sat at her feet.

Seeing her jeans and tank top, I belatedly noticed she'd changed clothes and irrational jealousy hit. Hard. "Did you let that fucker Talon into your apartment?" He didn't care who he fucked.

She glanced at the dogs, said something I couldn't hear and turned to walk away.

I slammed my fist into the doorframe. "You open this fucking door *right now*."

She stopped and glared. "Or what?"

I kicked at the piece of shit lock and the door popped open. Furious, desperate, I surged toward her.

She jumped back and one of the dogs rushed me. Ten pounds of barking, growling fury let loose. "Call him off," I warned.

"You broke the door!"

I didn't see it when she first appeared but I saw it now. Her eyes were red rimmed, her makeup smeared, her nose pink—my heart fucking sank. "You were crying."

She scooped up the canine menace and rushed around me to close the door. "I can't even secure it now." Her voice hitched up a notch. "How the hell am I going to keep the rain out?"

I stepped behind her and threw a top bolt she couldn't reach. Her scent hit me and I couldn't stop myself. I reached for her. "*Olivia—*"

Panic-laced hurt flooded her voice. "Don't you dare touch

me." She held the small dog to her chest while the other circled her feet. Her hair damp, her lip trembling, she looked scared as fuck.

It was a reality check and I softened my tone. "I'm not going to hurt you."

"You already did," she threw back.

Fuck this. I grasped the sides of her face, sank my fingers into her hair and threw down the one play I had. "I'm done." I didn't care about the money anymore. I didn't care about my five-year plan. I stared at the one woman who made me want more and I gave what I had to give. "I'm out." I didn't have one second of reservation. This moment had been coming. I could find another way to make money but I wouldn't find another her. I didn't give two fucks about any of those other women. I just wanted her.

She sucked in a breath. "I said. *Don't* touch me."

Low and controlled, her words took a moment to sink in. But when they did, it hit. Hard. Shit stabbed at my chest, my jaw ticked, but then my training kicked in. My back military straight, I shut down my expression and dropped my hands. "You're not staying here."

She nervously stepped back. "The dogs need me. They're scared."

I bent and picked up the pathetic mutt at her feet. "Bring them with you." I turned toward the door.

"You don't get to tell me what to do."

I spun and got in her face. I used my height as a weapon and my tone as ammunition. "The wind's picking up and these fucking windows won't hold past the hour." No way in hell was she staying here. "You have one minute to walk out of this shithole or I'm carrying you out." Whatever I had to do.

"You're not *carrying* me anywhere. And there's not just these two dogs."

God-fucking-dammit. "You think I'm going to let dogs come between you and your safety? How many?" I demanded.

She flinched and her attitude slipped. "One more. The other assistant spent all afternoon getting the other dogs out but Charlie's still in back. I can't move him."

I saw her fear. I saw she was worried about staying here, but I was still too pissed at her to do anything except storm past. I pushed the swinging door she'd come out of earlier and almost tripped on a mess of blankets at my feet.

Scarred, half shaved, a beast of an animal lay prone on the makeshift bed. Panting, looking like he was laboring to breathe, giant brown eyes looked up at me like he knew he was fucked. "Jesus Christ. What the hell happened to him?"

She squatted next to him and gently stroked his head. "Don't yell. He was hit by a car and left for dead." She kissed the mangy fur by his ear. "You're okay, sweet boy." He didn't even pick his head up.

People were fucking assholes. "Get these two." I set down the dog I was still holding. "I'll get him."

"You can't move him right now. He's in pain."

Motherfucker. "Either he comes with us or you leave him here. Decide right now because the parking lot's almost submerged and there's no way I'm letting you stay here."

"Oceanfront isn't any safer," she argued, but her tone said she wasn't going to push it.

"Reinforced steel, impact-resistant glass and shutters." I ticked off the list of hurricane countermeasures my penthouse boasted like a fucking selling agent. "It's a hell of a lot safer than this place. Take the two dogs and get in the car." I tipped my chin at the beast. "I'll put this one on your lap." I couldn't believe I was going to put three fucking dogs in my car.

"We won't all fit."

Another gust of wind roared outside and rattled the windows. "We'll make it work. Let's go."

She cupped the wounded animal's head. "Be a brave boy for me, Charlie. We're going for a ride." She gently wrapped the blankets around him, carefully tucking him in, then she glanced at me as she stood. "Don't let him get too wet."

The storm, our fight, all the bullshit in my head, it went silent and I stared at her.

The mouthy vixen with lush curves was there, but now there was also someone else. A woman beyond the grief of a lost brother, she stood and put a bottle of pills from the counter in her back pocket before scooping up two dogs. Adeptly holding them against her chest, she pulled an oversized raincoat off the back of the chair and threw it over all three of them. Determined and competent, she looked expectantly at me. "Ready?"

She was so fucking beautiful, my chest hurt.

"Yeah," I answered, my voice rough. I carefully picked up the beast and he let out a pathetic cry. "Shh, old boy, I got you."

Olivia hit the lights and held the swinging door open. "He's only two."

The damn dog looked like he was a hundred.

TWENTY-FOUR

Olivia

HE WAS HERE.

My heart in my throat, my hands shaking, I held Merry and Sparks to my chest and told myself not to stare.

His jaw set with determination, his hair wet, his shirt half-soaked and sticking to his huge biceps, Alex was the sexiest, most beautiful man I'd ever laid eyes on. The ache in my heart made me want to cry, but when he picked up Charlie like he was an infant, I wanted to forget what he did for a living.

Not wanting him to jostle Charlie or his stitches, I shoved a desk chair over to the front door and climbed up to undo the bolt he'd thrown. The wind gusted and pushed at the door like it couldn't wait to get in. Alex held his foot against the bottom frame to secure it until I stepped down, then he kicked the chair out of the way.

The door immediately blew open and rain pelted in.

Alex stepped against the open door so it didn't slam shut on me or the dogs. "Car's unlocked."

I grabbed three leashes and glanced at the useless lock on the glass door of the kennel. "I won't be able to secure the door after we leave."

"Doesn't matter. If the wind doesn't blow out the windows, the water will breach the door anyway." He nodded at his car. "Go."

I rushed to his fancy car and had to hold the door open against the wind. Merry struggled against me and Sparks whined as I slid into the leather seat. The second I tucked the two smaller dogs at my feet, Alex was there. Hunched over Charlie to protect him from the rain, he set the golden retriever on my lap. The heavy weight of him sank down on my thighs and he cried out.

"It's okay, sweet boy. Almost done." I cradled his head and Alex shut the door. By the time he crossed the front of the vehicle and got behind the wheel, he was soaked through.

Shoving his hair back and running his hands down his equally soaked thighs, he started the engine.

"I'm sorry about getting your seats wet." I glanced down at Charlie as Merry and Sparks huddled at my feet. "And the dogs in your car." He'd have hair everywhere.

Skirting the ever-growing flood in the kennel's parking lot, he didn't respond. He expertly maneuvered the car around a fallen branch as thick as my thigh and pulled onto the access road.

Tension cut through the small interior of the car and the dogs were quiet as Alex sped toward the main access road that cut east to his condo. Sheeting rain on the windshield, gusts biting into the car, Alex hit the last curve in the road then suddenly slammed on the brakes to avoid a fallen tree.

I grasped at Charlie as the car jolted but it wasn't enough. His poor broken body jerked in my arms and he howled in pain.

"*Fuck*, sorry." Alex spun the car around and glanced at the GPS map on the center console.

Fighting panic, I stroked Charlie's head. "There's another—"

"I see it. Hold on." He stepped on the gas and the car effortlessly shot down the road.

I didn't tell him the other end of the access road was low-lying, because we didn't have a choice. As we sped past the kennel, the last of the parking lot was already submerged and the front door was hanging at an odd angle. We were running out of time to get out of the flood zone.

Water crept up the sides of the road, and Alex kept the McLaren straddled over the middle lane marker. Trying not to panic so I didn't scare the dogs, I didn't realize I was holding my breath until we made it to the end of the road and I saw the turn onto the state road was passable. Air escaped my lungs as he pulled on to the main corridor.

Ignoring the traffic lights that still had power as they swayed dramatically, Alex sped toward the barrier island without stopping.

Halfway between the kennel and his place, he broke the tense silence. "How is he?"

I rubbed Charlie's ear. "Okay right now. His wounds are healing okay, but he still has broken ribs."

Alex didn't say anything else. Turning north on to US Highway 1, he maneuvered around the low-lying flooded areas and made his way to the south bridge for the barrier island. But as we got close, a police car with flashing lights was parked sideways, blocking access.

Alex pulled right up to the cruiser and lowered his window.

The cop dropped his window a few inches. "The bridge is closed, sir."

"I'm an island resident. La Mer Towers. I need to get home."

"Sorry, east side of the bridge is already flooded." He glanced at his watch. "They're closing the north bridge in fifteen minutes. You may have enough time."

Alex nodded and put the window up. Backing up, he spun the car around.

I nervously glanced at the clock on the dashboard. "Will we make it?"

"Six minutes," he clipped.

"You've timed it before?"

"I like to drive." He sped up.

My back pressed into the seat and I watched the clock instead of the angry, churning hurricane. Five minutes later, he pulled onto the access road for the north bridge. Police cars were parked on the street but they weren't blocking the bridge yet.

Alex flew past them.

We crested the top of the bridge and a giant gust of wind pushed the car into the next lane.

"*Alex.*" I clutched at Charlie as the barrier rushed my door.

He swerved the car back into the other lane. "We're fine."

My heart pounded as visions of us careening over the side of the bridge and plummeting into the Intracoastal flew through my mind. "Please, slow down," I begged.

He slowed, but only marginally. "You should've answered," he clipped as we hit the down slope of the bridge.

I held on to Charlie and glanced nervously out the window. "Answered what?"

"If you'd taken my call two hours ago, we'd already be in the penthouse."

I didn't argue, because right now, with the streets almost completely flooded and the winds tossing the car around, he was right. Except I'd never wanted to ride out a hurricane with him. A few hours ago, I wouldn't have felt safer anywhere else. But now? I told myself I was only here for the three ownerless dogs that didn't deserve to ride out a hurricane in a dilapidated kennel with shitty windows that a rich bitch was too cheap to fix. A rich bitch Alex had…. I sucked in a breath and shoved the thought away.

"Why'd you call Talon?"

The abrupt question caught me off guard. "I didn't. I called Jesse."

He turned south onto A1A. "Let me guess. Instead of taking care of you, he passed you off on Talon?"

I couldn't deny it, he was right. But after the stress and anxiety of the past couple hours, thinking about all the women he'd been intimate with and how it meant nothing to him, along with his attitude right now, I got mad. Seriously mad. "I didn't ask you to come get me. I didn't tell you to take in three homeless dogs. You showed up and told me to get in your car or else. You didn't even give me a choice. So cut the bullshit alpha attitude. I'm not riding out a hurricane with an asshole, and these dogs don't deserve any more stress in their lives." Merry was already a shaking mess at my feet. It was probably because she was cold, but still. She didn't ask for this. None of them had.

His jaw clenched and he took a sharp turn into his condo complex. The garage door opened as we approached and he pulled into a spot and cut the engine. His hand on the door handle, he spared me one glance. "I would never force you to do anything. You weren't safe at the kennel."

My heart twisted as he got out of the car. The silence of the garage after the howling of the wind only intensified the fact of where I was and who I was with.

When Alex opened my door, Sparks picked his head up and growled.

"Quit it." His authoritative command made Sparks instantly stop, and Alex reached for Charlie. "Easy, boy." He lifted him off my lap as gently as he could. "Grab the other two."

It occurred to me in that second that Alex wasn't bossy so much as commanding. Commanding like someone who was used to being in charge. Curiosity got the better of me. "What was your job in the military?"

"Recon," he said vaguely.

I scooped up the two little dogs and got out of the car as Alex headed for the stairs. "We're not taking the elevator?"

"If the power goes out, we'll be stuck." He held the door open with his foot.

I glanced at the elevator and sighed. Twenty floors. Shit. I took the first flight up then set Sparks down. "Come on, Sparks. Up you go." I nudged him and he sprang into action. Three seconds later, he was already a story ahead of me.

I silently trudged up with Merry, switching her from arm to arm every few floors. Halfway to the top, I took my jacket off and glanced over my shoulder. "You good?"

"Fine." Not even sweating, an expressionless mask in place, he didn't make eye contact.

"Awesome."

We didn't speak the rest of the way up. The only sound in the stairwell was Sparks's and my panting and the distant roar of the wind. By the time we hit the top floor, my thighs were burning. I held the door for Alex and he stepped sideways through.

"You want me to open the—" I started to offer to unlock his door but he was already ahead of me.

"Got it." He punched a code into a keypad next to the door. One click and the door swung open. "There's a linen closet down the hall. Grab some blankets." He walked into the living room with Charlie.

I set Merry down as Sparks flopped in the entryway. Noticing the paintings from the fundraiser were gone, I made my way down the hall with Merry on my heels. A closet the size of my kitchen had shelves neatly stacked with towels, sheets, blankets and one comforter. I grabbed two blankets and the comforter and squished my way back to the living room in my wet sneakers.

Waiting for me, Alex nodded toward the fireplace. "Right there."

Shooing Merry away, I dropped my jacket and the blankets and set the comforter down. "The paintings are gone."

"Guest room." He set Charlie down and he whined. Petting his head, he adjusted the blankets around him. "Have they eaten?"

I stepped out of my sneakers then put the two make-shift blanket beds next to Charlie. "Yeah, I fed them and took them out before you showed up." I stumbled over the last two words. Alex had come for me—through driving rain and hurricane-force winds, he'd come for me. I wanted to ignore what that did to my heart, but I couldn't. Sucking in a deep breath, knowing we were safe now, I fought the lump in my throat as Merry settled on the blanket closest to Charlie, and I whistled for the other dog. "Sparks, come." He trotted over and I patted his bed. "Lie down." I checked on Charlie. "You okay?" He licked my hand and I smiled. "Love you too, sweet boy." I stood and glanced at Alex.

His hands on his hips, he was staring at me.

Just like at the kennel, my heart skipped a beat and emotions swirled in my head. The tension between us was so thick, I could taste it, but my body didn't know he was a liar or that he sold himself, and it didn't care. Need pulsed between my legs and awareness shot up my spine. Worse, my chest ached just to feel his arms around me.

Sparks growled.

I looked over my shoulder and three tails thumped. I couldn't help it, I smiled. "Behave, Sparks." His tail wagged harder. Still smiling, I glanced at Alex. "Ignore him, he thinks he's badass."

Alex didn't smile. "Sparks?"

I nodded. "He's pretty feisty. And Merry is the little girl Terrier. She was left at the kennel the day before Christmas." Merry wagged her tail when she heard her name. "And Charlie you know." I sucked in a breath and told myself I could do this. I could talk about the dogs, make small talk, ride out the storm, then I'd leave in the morning. Mentally nodding to myself, I got down to tasks. "I need to get them some water."

"Bowls are in the kitchen. I'm going to close the shutters." No smile, no emotion, he went to the balcony.

Exhaling, I watched him through the wall of glass that caged in his living room. The muscles in his shoulders bulged as he pulled heavy accordion shutters across the length of the balcony, and I glanced at the dogs. "If we're lucky, a big gust will swamp him before he comes back inside." Sparks woofed in agreement. "My thoughts exactly."

I searched through the kitchen cupboards and filled three cereal bowls with water. Alex came back inside and the noise was noticeably less as he grabbed a remote off the wall and clicked through a series of buttons. Automatic shutters started sliding down over the windows.

I set the bowls down by the dogs. "Do you want me to fill a bathtub?" Assuming he had one.

"Why?" He put the remote back as his condo descended into an eerie, unnatural darkness.

"For water." If the power went off, chances were it'd also go off wherever the water supply came from, and when that happened, the city always put a boil water notice into effect. Not to mention, if the power was off, I wanted to still be able to flush a toilet.

"I have bottled." He disappeared down the hall.

"Ohh-kay." I squatted next to Charlie. "Come on, sweet boy." I held the water bowl close to his muzzle. "Drink something for me." His tongue halfheartedly lapped a few sips then he put his head back down. "I know, it sucks, but in a few hours, I can give you more medicine."

"What are you giving him?"

Startled, I jumped and some water sloshed out of the bowl. "Pain meds." I tried to wipe the floor with my already soaked tank top but I only spread the water around.

In dry shorts and a T-shirt, he held out some clothes. "Give me your jeans. I'll run them through the dryer before the power goes off."

My tank top stuck to me, my jeans damp from taking the dogs out to pee before he'd shown up at the kennel, I shivered and took the outstretched clothes. "Where should I—"

"Bathroom down the hall."

Intimidated by his mood, I simply nodded. I padded to the bathroom and shut the door. Even with all the shutters closed in his fortified castle, I could hear the wind and feel a slight sway in the building.

I ran my hand over the smooth granite of the bathroom counter and wondered just how safe his condo was. I didn't grow up with anything close to fancy shutters that closed with the touch of a button. My brother would put up the plywood we stored in the garage over all the windows and the house would get a new round of nail holes for his efforts. We would fill the bathtub and my mom would buy cereal and peanut butter and bread. Add a few random candles from the grocery store in tall glass jars with pictures of Jesus on them, and that was our hurricane preparedness.

My brother and I would play cards or board games, my mom would knit, and we'd sweat until the power came back on. But Alex's penthouse wasn't hot. It wasn't even warm. It felt like it was sixty-five degrees and there wasn't a corner that didn't have design thought put into it. Design that was paid for by....

I shook my head and whispered to myself, "Nope." Not going there.

A knock sounded on the door and I shoved the thoughts of exactly what he did for a living and Talon's justification of it down deep. "Yeah?"

"Give me your clothes. If you want a shower with hot water, you should take one before the power goes out."

"Just a sec." I quickly stripped and folded my shirt and underwear into the jeans. Grabbing a towel off the rack, I wrapped it around me and cracked the door. "Here you go. And thanks." I held my arm out but he didn't take the clothes. "What's wrong? Are the kids okay?"

"Kids?" His voice sounded off. Strained.

"The dogs."

"Fine."

My arm suspended, my muscles took notice. "Alex?"

When he didn't answer, I opened the door wider.

Achingly beautiful blue eyes stared down at me. "Did he touch you?"

I didn't have to ask who. "No." Talon had walked me to my apartment and watched me with a silence that reminded me of my brother as I'd grabbed a change of clothes and my phone charger. Then he'd driven me to the kennel, took one look at the place and said I shouldn't stay there. I told him I wasn't moving Charlie, and he'd reluctantly dropped me off.

Alex's exhaled breath whispered across my skin and gooseflesh crawled up my neck. For one impossible moment, I felt it. An invisible tether wound so tight around my heart, it ended and began with him. I wasn't truly living until I'd met him. I was drowning in grief and guilt, and the life I'd been breathing, it ended when he'd kissed me for the first time. But now that I knew what he was, I couldn't see a future anymore and my past was suddenly buried too deep to give me solace.

I was adrift. And the man standing next to me wasn't the anchor.

Alex Vega was the storm.

TWENTY-FIVE

Alex

DON'T DO IT. WALK AWAY. TAKE THE FUCKING clothes and walk. *Away.*

I didn't fucking walk.

I opened my mouth like a goddamn pussy and shit in my head bled out.

"Judge all you want. I won't apologize for who I am." Not to her, not to anyone.

She blinked. "I'm not judging you."

"That's exactly what you're doing. The second you found out I slept with women for money, you condemned me." *Slept.* Past tense. Past fucking tense because that's what she'd done to me.

"I was angry that you lied."

"I didn't lie. You didn't ask." I'd never fucking lied to her.

She lowered her arm. "Alex...."

It wasn't the four letters she said when she was drenching my dick in her come. It wasn't even a name. It was a fucking condescending insult, and I lost it. "The size of my dick and wallet was good enough for you last night." I ruthlessly held her gaze. "Then you found out you weren't the only woman who'd come on my cock." Goddamn, I was pissed. "I can't have

199

a past? You're the only one allowed to have one?"

"Stop it." She held the towel to her chest.

"Stop what? Stop asking you why it's okay for you to have fucked other guys before we met but it's not okay for me to have fucked other women?"

"You're being an ass, and that's not what you asked, nor is that what this is about."

"Isn't it?" I was done holding back. What the fuck did I have to lose now? "You can fuck Talon or your asshole friend, but I couldn't fuck your boss?"

She flinched and went even paler.

"Which part bothers you the most? That your boss paid three grand to suck my dick? Or that I got off on it?" Goddamn, I was fucking pissed.

"Fuck you!" She stepped back and tried to slam the door.

I shoved my foot forward and the door flew back open as I grasped her arm. "You think you're too good for someone like me? You think I'm fucking damaged? Tainted? *Diseased*?" My anger hit a fucking plateau and kept going.

"Let me go!" she cried.

"Guess what?" I propelled her back until her ass hit the wall. "I'm no fucking prince, but you're the *only* woman I ever gave a damn about!" I threw her arm out of my grasp, ripped her clothes from her hand and fucking stormed out.

I tossed her clothes in the dryer and practically tripped on a ten-pound terrier that looked like a goddamn overgrown rat. "What the fuck are you doing out of bed?"

The little dog cowered.

"*God-fucking-dammit.*"

She started to shake.

I shoved my hands through my wet hair. "Go lie down."

She lay down. Right fucking there.

Motherfucking *fuck, fuck, fuck.* I scooped the dog up. "This is why I don't fuck with women." She pressed into me and licked my hand, the little bitch.

I grabbed the fucking crate I kept hurricane shit in and carried it to the kitchen counter. Fuming, at her, at myself for saying the shit I'd said, I put the damn dog in the kitchen sink and grabbed a case of water out of the pantry.

Strolling into the kitchen in my T-shirt and sweats that she'd rolled up around her hips, Olivia went to the sink. "She can't get down from here."

I dumped the water on the counter next to the crate. "I know." Nippy little rat could fucking stay there. She was all over my shit.

Olivia leaned over and scratched the dog behind her ears. "This is too high up for you, sweetheart, isn't it? You're too little to jump down."

Her perfect fucking ass was aimed at me and I growled in frustration. "Then take her down."

She scooped the dog up and held her up to her face. "Mean ole daddy. I'll let you down." The dog licked her face and she bent to put her down.

Fucking *daddy.* I threw her shit right back on her. "She doesn't pay me to be her *daddy.*"

Olivia froze. Then she sucked in air, set the dog down and straightened her back. "No, I guess she doesn't."

I snorted. "Go ahead." Polite didn't suit her. "Fucking ask." My cell vibrated in my pocket, but I ignored it and turned the oven on.

"I don't know what you're talking about." She crossed her arms protectively around herself.

It fucking pissed me off. "Don't bullshit me. You know exactly what I'm saying." I pulled chicken and turkey bacon out of the fridge. "Ask whatever the hell you want."

She didn't even pretend to think about it. "Is that what your clients do? They pay you to pretend to be their daddy?" The question couldn't spew out of her mouth fast enough.

I threw the meat on the counter then I caged her in. Aggressive, dominant, I stared her down. "You want to know what my clients *paid* me to do?" I didn't wait for an answer. "You want to know how I earned my fee?"

She tried to lean back.

I hovered closer. "I made them feel special." I traced the line of her jaw. "I made them feel wanted." I grasped her chin and lowered my voice. "I made them feel good about themselves." Then I took their fucking money because not one of them knew what it meant to grow up like I did or come home from Afghanistan with your head so fucked-up you wanted to go back.

"Why?" she barely whispered.

I wasn't her brother. I wasn't six feet under. I had all my body parts and I was fucking present, so I wasn't about to complain. "Because I could."

Her gaze held mine. "There's more."

That was it. Right fucking there. Clients took what they wanted, every last orgasm. They didn't give a shit about me. But this woman? Five foot nothing, challenging my lies when she wouldn't even take my help during a hurricane, let alone my money? I shook my head. "You shouldn't have tried to take those paintings back." She had no clue what she'd set in motion.

Her shoulders straightened. "You shouldn't have bought them all."

"I'd do it a thousand times over if it meant I got to see you pissed off about it." Because that's when I fucking fell for her, and I was desperate enough right then to tell her that. "Wanna know why?" I pressed my hips into hers and dragged my thumb across the soft skin of her neck because that's what I did. I made women want me. Every move was choreographed. Every touch had a purpose. My body was the weapon and my attitude the trigger.

She sucked in a breath. "What are you doing?"

Good fucking question. What was I doing? Because for the first time in three years, I had no fucking clue. I sucked in a breath and pushed away from her. "Making you dinner." My cell vibrated again, and I stupidly didn't look at the display before I answered. "What?"

"I cannot stay here alone. There is a hurricane."

Christ. "That house is built like a fucking bunker. You're fine."

"The wind is too strong. It will break the windows. Trees are hitting them."

"Put the shutters down."

"I am not going out in this."

I sighed. "You don't have to. Go to the kitchen, by the far wall. See the remote?" I glanced at Olivia as I pulled stuff for a salad out of the fridge, but she was playing with the girl dog.

"I don't see it."

Jesus. "Look around, Irina. You're not fucking helpless."

"I see no remote... oh. What am I supposed to do with this?"

Jesus Christ, is this what her husband put up with? "Cycle through the settings until it says *all*. Then hit the bottom button. The shutters will close." My cell buzzed with another call. "Hold on." I glanced at the display. Dane. "Where are you?"

Wind roared in the background. "All the lights are on in my house."

No fucking shit. "You said I could use it for three days. What are you doing, standing outside?" The crazy fuck, I wouldn't put it past him.

"In the driveway. Who is it?"

I glanced at Olivia, but her back was to me now. "Irina."

"The client."

Olivia was listening, I knew she was. I didn't have shit to hide at this point, but I didn't want to broadcast either. I chose my words. "I'm out." Dane would pick up on it.

Pause. Then, "You quit."

"Yeah."

"Because of the woman in my house?"

"Unrelated."

"Another woman," he stated.

I didn't deny it. "I thought you were out of town for a few days."

"Plans changed."

Secretive fuck. "She's on the other line. What do you want me to tell her?"

"She stable?"

Any other business, any other person asking, I would've wondered what the fuck he was getting at. Unfortunately, I knew exactly what he meant. We'd all had to dump unstable clients. "Yeah. Just spoiled as fuck. You deal with this, I'll owe you."

"You already owe me."

I got it. He didn't like people at his house, not while he was there. We were similar in that way. Our homes were our sanctuaries, and now mine had a woman and three dogs in it. "I'll tell her she has twenty-four hours."

"Copy. Parameters?"

Dane had left the military, but he'd always be a Marine. He spoke in code half the time, and life was a series of executable tasks to him. I knew what he was asking, and he could fuck her for twenty-three of those twenty-four hours for all I cared. "None."

"Tell her I'm coming in through the garage."

"Done. Thanks." I clicked back over to Irina. "The guy who owns the house is there. He's coming in through the garage. Don't shoot him." I doubt she had a gun, but who fucking knew?

"What? No! You promised me, Alex. You said you would come get me."

"No," I warned. "I never said that. I'm doing you this one favor then you have to deal with your own shit."

"But—" She sucked in a shocked breath. "Who are you?" she snapped.

"Dane." Dane's rough voice carried through the phone. "Tell Vega all clear."

I almost felt sorry for her. Dane was a big motherfucker. "I heard him. Don't be a pain in the ass. He's doing you a solid."

"Alex." She said my name in a panic.

"You're fine. You'll be safe with him." For the most part.

"Hang up," Dane clipped.

I smirked. "Bye, Irina." I ended the call and shoved my phone back in my pocket.

"Friend?" Olivia didn't look up from petting the dog.

I exhaled. "Former client."

"You sound like… you're friends with her."

"Not friends." I took out a baking pan.

Olivia frowned. "But she's calling you?"

I wasn't going to lie to her, but I also didn't feel like I had to explain myself. "Her husband kicked her out. She needed a place to land. A friend of mine was out of town, so I took her to his place."

"She's married and she's your client?"

The judgment was laced through her question thicker than the bacon I was wrapping around the chicken. "Her husband was older and he knew."

"So that makes it okay? That's still adultery."

"Not my problem." Not anymore.

"You come between a husband and a wife and you think it's not your problem?"

I wrapped the last chicken breast, washed my hands and threw the pan in the oven. "A guy on a diet goes to a fast food joint and orders a burger. Is that the restaurant's fault? No. They simply provided the commodity. They didn't tell the guy to cheat on his diet."

She held firm to her bullshit. "They may as well have."

"How? By selling a basic human necessity?" I grabbed a cutting board and a knife and dumped them in front of her. "Make the salad."

She didn't move. "You're comparing food to sex?"

"We need to eat to live and fuck to procreate." Both necessities. I measured out some rice and water and put it in the microwave.

She watched my movements. "Now you're selling sperm?"

"No." Not that I ever considered it. "Far less profitable.

Which is a sad reflection on society." I crossed my arms and leaned on the counter opposite her. "Salad isn't going to make itself."

She glanced at my arms then inhaled. "So you helped her."

I was vain enough to flex my biceps. "Yes." I wanted her looking at me.

"That was… nice of you." She dropped her gaze.

I closed the distance between us because I couldn't fucking leave her alone. "I'm not an asshole."

Her arms tightened around herself and her voice got quieter. "I know."

"Do you?" It took everything I had not to touch her.

TWENTY-SIX

Olivia

IT TOOK EVERYTHING I HAD NOT TO REACH FOR HIM. HE smelled so good, like soap and promise, and I wanted those ridiculously huge arms around me. Every passing second, it was harder to hold on to my indignation, and if I were being honest, I understood why he hadn't told me what he was. Drunk or not, revenge or lust, I never would've slept with him after the fundraiser.

I turned my back to him and stared at the cutting board. I hated that a client was calling him. I hated it a thousand times worse than anything I'd ever felt when I saw Jesse with Jennifer.

"You gonna answer me?"

My eyes closed and I breathed in. Even his voice was sexy. Deep, but not loud, he could drag me under just whispering my name. "What was the question?" I knew what it was.

His hands landed on either side on me on the counter and his breath touched my neck. "Do you know what your problem is?"

Besides the fact I'd fallen so hard for him it hurt? "I don't know how to cook?"

He inhaled. "You're jealous."

I was. And I had too many questions to count, but one stood out more than any other. "Why me?" I picked the knife up. "You could have any woman you want."

He took the knife from me and turned me around. "You're seriously asking why I want you? After you felt what we were like together?"

Heat flamed my cheeks and I dropped my gaze.

He lowered his voice. "Look at me, Olivia."

Hesitant and vulnerable, I looked up.

His deep blue gaze held mine. "Do you know what it feels like to be inside you?"

I bit my bottom lip and shook my head.

"Like I'm fucking home."

I sucked in a breath and fought tears, but he wasn't finished.

"Like every other bullshit moment in life is wasted energy. When I'm inside you, the rest disappears. I know you feel that connection. It's more than every way I can make you come. I've fucked enough women. I know the difference. Sex is sex. But with you?" His expression so intense he looked angry, he shook his head. "It's like coming home."

A tear slid down my cheek.

His hand came up, but then he made a fist and dropped it. "I told you I'm not playing games," he ground out. "I'm not giving up my clients for you. I'm giving them up because I don't need them." His nostrils flared with an inhale. "I knew this day was coming. I planned for it. But the timeline?" He stared at me. "That's all you. I'm not going back. I don't *want* to go back."

It was everything and nothing I wanted to hear. My heart broke as much as it soared, but I didn't know what to say. I didn't even know what to think. I felt guilty for being angry with him at his past, but God, I wanted to fall into his arms because he felt more like home than anything in the past two years had.

But when I didn't say anything, he shook his head and stepped back.

I panicked. "What do you want me to say?"

He took the rice out of the microwave. "Whatever you want."

He was defensive now. "That's not fair." I couldn't believe I was having this conversation. I'd known him hours, *hours*, but the crazy part was it didn't even seem weird. "I'm allowed to be confused. I'm allowed to feel whatever I want."

"I'm not the fucking emotion police." He opened the oven and used tongs to flip the chicken.

The scent of the turkey bacon he'd wrapped the chicken in filled the air. "No, but you act like all you have to do is say a few words and everything should be fine. Life doesn't fall into place like that." It never did. My brother was dead, my mother was in another state pretending she'd never had kids, and I'd fucked a guy who charged women for sex.

"I'm not holding shit back from you. You want to make that complicated, that's on you." He shut the oven door and pushed me aside to get at the lettuce. Quick and methodical, he chopped lettuce, tomatoes and cucumbers, then threw it all into two bowls.

Now I was angry. "What do you want me to say? I forgive you? I don't care about your past? Even if I did say those things now, it wouldn't matter. You're pissed that I didn't give you whatever response you expected." My voice whiney, I sounded pathetic and needy.

He grabbed two plates out of the cupboard and practically slammed them on the counter, but he didn't say anything. Silverware followed then he took two beers out of the fridge. He popped both caps off and handed me a bottle without looking at me.

I took it. "You going to say something?"

"Dinner's almost ready. Napkins are in the drawer by the fridge." He checked the chicken again.

I yanked the drawer open. Linen, real linen napkins, all neatly folded and perfectly pressed, lined the front of the drawer. I took two and resisted the urge to wrinkle the hell out of them before I grabbed the silverware he'd taken out. I set two settings at the stools on the other side of the kitchen island then I sat my ass down and took a sip of beer. It had some stupid Belgian label and of course it was the best-tasting beer I'd ever had.

Confused, still pissed off, and about a thousand other emotions, I settled in to stare as he took the chicken out of the oven and plated it along with the rice. Except he didn't just plate it, he moved as if every step was choreographed to make him look like the sex god he was. His muscles flexed, his shoulders stretched, even the set to his jaw was sexy. Then he slid our plates across the island like he was a cooking show pro and set one bowl of salad by each of us with a flourish.

Every second of his little act made me angrier.

"I know what you're doing," I accused.

He sat down next to me and took a sip of his beer, but he didn't respond.

Arrogant prick. "Where's the salad dressing?"

He took another swig of beer. "Don't have any. Never use it."

Who the hell didn't use salad dressing? "It's eat or consume, not *use*. Salt, pepper?"

"You don't need it." He picked up his knife and fork and cut into his meat. "I seasoned the chicken before I baked it." He calmly took a bite.

I yanked his napkin off the counter and held it up in front of him, then I wrinkled that fucker into a ball. Once I'd decimated the ironing job that napkin had gone through, I shook it out and threw it on his lap. "Don't forget your napkin."

His second bite almost to his mouth, he paused only a fraction of a second. "Thanks." Then he popped the chicken in and chewed.

Not the reaction I'd been hoping for, I jabbed the fork in the meat and hacked off a chunk with the knife. "How'd you know where I was?" Suddenly starving, I shoveled the bite in. Holy shit it was good.

"Talon."

I'd figured as much. "Why'd you come for me?" I cut off another too-big bite and chowed it down.

"You don't want me to answer that. How's your chicken?"

"You know it's delicious. And yes, I do want you to answer."

"Good." He ate three forkfuls of dry salad.

"Why don't you *use* dressing?"

"Empty calories." Two more huge bites and he finished off the salad.

I put my fork down. "Seriously?" He was one of those guys?

He nodded at my plate. "Eat. And yes, seriously."

Disheartened, I picked my fork up. "It never would've worked between us." I loved food. All kinds of food.

"It'll work perfectly."

"*Worked*, past tense." I tried a bite of salad. It sucked.

"Work. Present tense," he argued. "I told you, you didn't want to know why."

The wind kicked up and one of the dogs cried. I glanced behind us, but they were all on their blankets. "Why what?"

"Why I came for you." He ate his last bite of chicken and downed the rice in three bites.

"Because you're crazy?" Normal people didn't go driving in hurricanes.

"No, because you're mine." He stood to clear his plate and the power went out.

213

TWENTY-SEVEN

Alex

ONE OF THE DOGS STARTED CRYING AND OLIVIA'S FORK hit the counter a second before her stool scraped across the floor.

It was black as pitch, and I couldn't see shit. "Hold up."

"I'm going to the dogs. They're scared."

Jesus Christ, she was stubborn. "They'll be even more scared if you trip on them. Wait one second." I pulled my phone out and used the light from the screen to get to the crate on the counter. Three seconds later, I had the battery-operated lanterns lit. "Here." I handed her one. "Put this by the dogs while I clean up."

She took the lantern, and I cleared the dishes. The wind kicked up and it sounded like a fucking freight train was going directly over the building. I hastily washed up, and when I cleared the napkins, I fucking smiled. It'd taken an act of God not to laugh my ass off when she'd crumpled that shit in front of me.

I grabbed our beers and another lantern and headed to the living room, but she was on the phone.

"You're cutting in and out. I can't hear you... I said I was fine. Me and the dogs are at La Mer.... I know.... I know... what?" She looked at the phone and swore then hung up.

214

"The boyfriend?" I put her beer and the lantern on the coffee table and sank into the couch. "Didn't want to tell him who you were with?" The small female dog got up and came to my feet.

"He knows who I'm with, and for the hundredth time, he's not my boyfriend. He already has a girlfriend." She snatched her beer and drank half.

"And he kissed you?" I chuckled, even though it still pissed me off. "Who's the player now?" I looked at the pathetic bitch at my feet. Her tail wagged.

Olivia sneered at me. "At least he only has one girlfriend."

"As opposed to my many clients?" I knew what she wanted to know, but I wasn't going to make it easy on her. I'd already said too fucking much. She could work for it if she wanted to know about me. The dog nudged my leg, and I picked it up and dumped it on the couch next to me.

"You said it, not me."

The dog got on my lap and settled in. I scratched it behind the ears as I finished my beer, but I didn't bother replying. I should've been telling myself it was a mistake to go after her, power through the night, and then dump her and her fucking mutts off. But even knowing I probably didn't have a chance in hell with her, I'd still rather sit here in the dark with three smelly dogs and spar with her than be anywhere else. And it didn't escape my notice that, same as me, she would've ridden out the storm alone if I hadn't come for her.

The storm raged and we sat quiet.

Two days ago, I didn't know there was a hurricane or an Olivia Toussaint. Right at this moment, they were one and the same.

Fuck, I was tired. Three years tired. I leaned my head back.

She broke our silence. "What did you do after your first client?"

I picked my head up and looked at her. The lantern throwing shadows on the angles of her face, she was so damn beautiful, she could be a model. "What do you mean?" I knew what she meant.

She shrugged like it was a casual question. "I don't know. Like after, were you upset or something?"

I got my fucking dick sucked. Twice. "I'm not a goddamn PBS documentary. I took my money and bought a suit." What the hell did she think I'd done? Rock in a goddamn corner?

"I'm not an idiot. I didn't think you'd cry in your Cheerios. I was just…." She sighed. "Whatever, forget it."

I leaned my head back, wondering why the fuck I'd told her she could ask me anything. Worst fucking mistake ever. "I had a suit made because rack shit never fit, then I paid my rent."

"That's it?"

"I charged the shoes and belt." I'd figured I'd make it back in one night, and I did. Ten-fold.

She laughed. "You're so fucking vain."

Women liked to look at me. Always had. I just gave them a reason to appreciate me. That was the difference. I changed the subject. "Why didn't Bob the Builder buy into your charity? Or fund it?" Now that I knew who he was, I knew he made bank. Not as much as me, but enough that he could've helped her.

She inhaled then let it out slowly, and I could almost feel her breath. Fuck, I wanted to touch her.

"I told him not to," she admitted.

"And he listened?"

"Yep."

"What a fucking pussy."

"Why? Because he did what I asked him to do? Being decent doesn't make him a *pussy*."

Yes, it did. "He's a fucking pussy for not doing what was right by you."

"Since when is someone else paying for your dreams 'doing right' by them?" She put air quotes around *doing right*.

"He wanted to fuck you, he wanted to keep you, but he stepped back and watched from the sidelines like a spectator?" Fucking absurd was what this conversation was. "He's a pussy." I couldn't explain it any better than that.

"You're an ass."

Maybe. But I wouldn't have left her adrift. "I would've done shit to help." I pet the stupid rat's head that was asleep on my lap like she'd never had it better.

Olivia scoffed. "Right. Because cleaning out kennels is right up your alley."

"More than one way to help a woman besides shoveling shit." But if she'd asked me at this point, I probably would've done it.

"I'm sure all your clients *love* your help."

Goddamn it. "I told you I was out."

"Good for you."

Fuck this. "How many men you slept with?"

"None of your business." She stretched her legs out in front of her like a dancer.

"Give me the fucking number, sweetness." Damn, I loved to watch her move.

"You don't get to call me that."

"I'll call you whatever the hell I want. How many?"

"Nice try." She crossed her arms.

That meant one of two things. She was either rocking her college years or she was locked up tight. And since I knew exactly how tight she was, I had my answer. "Two," I guessed.

"What's this going to prove if you find out how many men I've slept with?"

"It's not going to prove shit."

"Then why ask?"

"Why not answer?" It was less than five, I'd bet my McLaren on it. "Three."

"No."

I egged her on. "You embarrassed?"

"It was four, okay, *four*. You happy?"

Not by a long shot. I hated those four fuckers. "How old were you when you lost your virginity?"

"Oh my God, *what the hell*? I'm not telling you that."

"Sixteen?"

She looked pissed.

Shit. "Fifteen?" *Damn.*

"I was nineteen, asshole."

"A guy a year on average." I took a sip of my beer. "I fucked Kristie Peterson after a football game when I was seventeen."

Her eyes went wide with curiosity. "You played football?"

Christ, she was a trip. "Yeah, I played." My grades were shit, I'd needed to be good at something. "But that's not the point. I enlisted after high school, and for the next three years, I fucked Kristie every time I had leave. We parted ways when she wanted more. I spent the next six years neck-deep in the Marines then I got out and started fucking for money. Do you know how many clients total I had?" I didn't wait for an answer. "Twenty-four. Add the few women I messed around with after Kristie and that's thirty-one. Two-point-eight women a year." I let that sink in a moment. "You want to fucking condemn me for taking money for sex, fine. But don't act like I fucked my way through hundreds of women."

She blinked.

I fucking knew it. She thought I was a manwhore, and I was, but only in the literal sense. I shook my head, dumped the little dog on the floor and stood.

"Alex."

Fuck. I hated how my heart jumped every damn time she said my name. "What?" She didn't answer, so I turned and looked down at her. Except it wasn't just her, three pairs of eyes were staring up at me.

"Why?"

Her voice quiet, the tone was too fucking close to sympathy for comfort, so I bit out a response. "Money."

"You could've earned it another way." There wasn't a hint of judgment in her tone, but I took it that way.

"Don't talk to me about money unless you came from nothing." Money was always the bottom line, especially if you had none.

Inhaling, she nodded like she understood. "Safety net, nest egg, I get it."

No, she didn't. But that was my fault because I'd only told her half the truth. I wasn't sharing the rest of that shit. No way. I went for another beer and Merry followed, dancing at my feet the whole damn way.

I closed the fridge and Olivia was right there, holding the rat dog close like she needed protection. "She probably needs to go out."

I opened the beer, threw the cap on the counter and stared at her as I drank.

She held my gaze for half a second then glanced around the kitchen. "So…."

I stared at her lips.

She licked them. "We can't go outside yet."

Wind thrashed at the shutters and rattled the hell out of them. I stared at her neck.

She swallowed and her voice turned quieter. "Probably not for a while."

My gaze swept over her tits.

She shifted the dog to the other hip. "Say something."

I leveled her with a look. "I'm done talking."

"Oh-kay, well, that's going to make for a long—"

"Put the dog down."

She bent and did what I'd said, but when she straightened, she crossed her arms. "She needs to pee."

I didn't care if the damn thing pissed on the floor. I'd just realized my mistake with her, and I was going to test my fucking theory. "You trust me," I stated.

Her mouth popped open. "I…." She stopped like she had to think about it.

I had her. "Go ahead. It's not a question, but answer it."

Her thighs pressed together and her chest rose and fell twice then her hands went to her hips. "I never said I didn't trust you, but you lied."

I set my beer down. "Turn around."

"What?"

"Hands on the counter."

"If you think for one minute I'm going to let you—"

"*Now.*"

She turned. *She fucking turned.* My dick already straining at my shorts, I stepped up to her back, but I didn't fucking touch her. "What else did I say?"

Her hands went to the counter.

My eyes closed, air filled my lungs and relief like I'd never known hit me in the chest. But this wasn't the victory I wanted.

A fraction of a breath away, my mouth so close to her skin I could taste her, I spoke. "You want me touching you, commanding you. You want what I can do for your body. Your thighs are pressed together, your pulse is racing, you're aching for it. You want me buried so fucking deep, you forget your name." But that was never the problem.

"*Alex.*" Breathless, my name wasn't an order, it was a plea.

The hurricane raging outside, turmoil churning in my gut, I threw down the ultimatum. "I touch you now, it's for keeps." I stepped back.

Her chest rose, her shoulders stiffened, and her hands gripped the granite counter. "That's not fair."

"Life's not fair. Decide."

Waves thrashed the shore, hundred-mile-an-hour winds hit the building, but she didn't say shit.

I picked up my beer and one of the lanterns, and I walked out.

TWENTY-EIGHT

Olivia

MY HEART POUNDING, MY BODY ACHING, I SHOOK.
I wanted him. I wanted him more than I'd ever wanted anything. The way he touched me, the way he held me, his voice, his strength, he made me feel like I mattered. He was more valuable than his past. I knew that.

I was standing before I realized I'd gotten up.

I was walking before I knew my feet were moving.

I was following the light.

Across the living room, down the hall, a soft glow filtered out of the laundry room.

I stopped in the doorway.

Vulnerability tumbled from my mouth. "What happens when another client calls?"

My clothes in his hands, he stilled. "You trust me."

"What if I don't know how?" Everyone I'd ever trusted let me down.

Methodical and precise, he folded my jeans. "You do it anyway."

"What do you do?"

He turned. Shadows cast across the angles of his face, the

hurricane raged outside, and my world fell away to only one thing.

"I want this to be real," I whispered.

His hands cupped my face, his body heat surrounded me and his lips covered mine. Crashing, falling, spiraling into the depth of my fears, I let go.

And he caught me.

Achingly tender, he held me. Searching the heat of my mouth, as if he needed me to breathe, he gave. Reverence, desire, need, he gave me what he had to give. With a truth no words could touch, he kissed me until the fear slipped away and a new truth seeded deep in my soul.

His lips against mine, he gave me hope. "This is real."

"Alex," I begged.

"You're mine." He pulled back just enough for me to see his intent gaze. "I'm yours."

I needed more than words. "Show me."

He swept me up into his arms and grabbed the lantern.

Without speaking, he carried me into his bedroom. The lantern was hastily left on the dresser as long shadows disappeared into dark corners, and a man I never dreamed would steal my heart set me on his bed.

Pulling his shirt over his head, then dropping his shorts, he ripped my clothes off and crawled up my body with desperate need. An Alex I'd never met pushed my legs apart and surged. Caging me in, rushing me, gripping two handfuls of my hair, he sank his tongue into my mouth. And more volatile than the storm outside, we collided. His hands, his mouth, his tongue all over my body, he stole my heart and silenced my fears.

I grabbed on to the tight muscles of his ass and pulled.

A growl ripped from his chest as the head of his cock met my tight heat. Then he went perfectly still.

Hovering, suspended at my entrance, he sucked in a labored breath, then another. "*Olivia.*" As if dragged across gravel, my name was a snarl of a command I didn't understand.

"Please," I begged.

Blue eyes the color of midnight looked fiercely down at me. "Decide."

My breath caught.

This was it.

This was my hope. This was my fear. This was my chance.

Happiness wasn't a choice. It was opportunity. Life had stolen my heart, but fate was giving me this moment to take it back. To take him. To let him take me. There was only one condition.

All or nothing.

I didn't have to think about it.

Breathing in, my knees came up and my feet braced on the bed. My heart racing, my movements slow, deliberate, I raised my hips until our bodies became one and Alex sank inside me.

Sucking air past his teeth, his hard length pushed to my cervix. He gripped my hip and held me still. "You're so goddamn beautiful. I wanna be inside you forever."

Words I never thought I would give away again ached to come out, but I held back. "Don't break my heart," I whispered.

His hand caught my face and his unwavering gaze cut to my soul. "Never." He pulled back then thrust forward, deep and slow, grinding his hips against mine.

I held on to his strong arms. "*Alex.*"

"Right here, sweetness, right here." He stroked deep inside me. "You feel that?"

Oh my God. I started to unravel. "Yes."

"That's it, beautiful." He kissed my neck, my throat. "Let it go." Rhythmic, controlled, he stroked in and out of me.

Swirls of desire licked up my spine, building until my muscles started to constrict around him and my head fell back. My eyes fluttered shut and need crawled out of my chest.

"Christ," he groaned.

My arms and legs started to shake. I was sinking and I was flying but I couldn't fall over that edge. Not without him. "I need you," I panted. "With me." *Oh God.*

Huge hands gripped my face. "Eyes on me," he demanded.

I looked up.

Dark, hooded, fierce, his penetrating stare stole my breath. "You look at me when you come."

The orgasm started to erupt in a thousand points of pleasure so intense it was painful. "*Alex.*"

"Feel me come inside you." His gaze locked on mine, he thrust hard one more time, then stilled.

He released his desire inside me, and together, we fell over the edge.

TWENTY-NINE

Alex

THE HURRICANE RAGING, HER BODY WRAPPED TIGHT IN
my arms, I watched her fall asleep.

The whole fucking world could disappear outside
and I wouldn't give a single damn.

I had her.

I had the woman I never knew I wanted. And I was fucking
keeping her. I touched my lips to her forehead, and she inno-
cently turned into me. My eyes closed, and it felt like I'd only
been asleep for seconds when something cold and wet nudged
the back of my arm.

I opened one eye. The lantern still on, I glanced over my
shoulder.

The little bitch dog stood on the bed, wagging her tail.

I groaned and she licked my face before nudging me again.

I'd never had a dog but I got the fucking gist. Slow, so I
didn't wake her, I untangled myself from Olivia and rolled out
of bed. I pulled shorts on and glanced at my bedside clock, but
the power was still off.

I pulled my T-shirt over my head and realized the sound
of the wind had diminished to gusts. "Come on," I quietly told
the dog.

I grabbed a flashlight from the crate in the kitchen and glanced at the other two dogs, but both were sleeping. Scooping Merry up, I left the front door cracked and jogged down the twenty flights. We hit the lobby, and while it was still dark out, I could tell the hurricane was on its way out. I picked the closest patch of green and set the little dog down.

She immediately peed. Then she jumped up on my leg with her front paws.

"You done? You need to take a shit or something, do it now. I'm not coming back down in an hour." Jesus Christ, I was talking to a fucking dog.

She wagged her tail, and I swore to God she fucking smiled at me.

I shook my head and scooped her up. A few minutes later, we were back in the penthouse and I set her down. "Now go to bed." I pointed to her blanket.

She trotted over and flopped down then curled into a ball.

I chugged a water, grabbed one for Olivia, then made my way back to bed and pulled her back into my arms.

"Alex?"

God, I loved the sound of her voice. "Right here, beautiful. Go back to sleep."

She turned into me and her breathing evened out.

Peace settled in my heart and I was out in minutes.

The second time I was woken up, it was my cell phone vibrating on the nightstand.

My clock blinking, the power back on, I glanced at the caller ID and sighed as I answered. "Hold up." I looked reluctantly at lush curves and smooth skin as I got out of bed. I didn't have shit to hide from Olivia, but I also didn't want to have this conversation in front of her. I quietly closed the door behind me and made my way toward the kitchen. "You fucking asshole, you did that on purpose."

Jared laughed. "You're right. I had to see what woman you were giving it up for."

I wanted to hate him, but I wasn't a fucking pussy. I owned who I was. "I'm not giving up shit." Olivia wasn't a sacrifice.

He smirked. "So you're taking clients again?"

Not a chance in hell. "No, you are." I used the remote to open all the shutters except the ones in the master bedroom.

He laughed again. "I'm taking the day off, bro. After last night, I'm gonna need Astroglide for a week."

Christ. "Learn to pace yourself." I stepped out onto the balcony and opened the accordion shutters.

"I did pace myself, for eight hours straight through a damn hurricane."

I could practically see his smug smile. Fucking idiot. "I'm sending you my schedule and contact list. Don't wait to make contact with all of the clients. Confirm the dates and let them know you're—"

"Whoa, whoa, whoa, bro. I got my own clients."

"Now you have twenty more." If he kept them all, which he wouldn't. "They all pay bank, so weed your shit out."

Silence.

Debris covered the beach, but shockingly none of the palm trees around the pool area were down. "Jared?"

"Are you fucking serious?" he scoffed. "You're throwing your shit away for what? *Love?*"

The single word, ground out like it was the holy grail of sins, hit me.

Jared didn't wait for me to answer. "You think that shit's gonna last? Two weeks, tops, and the honeymoon's over."

"You don't know what you're talking about. Shut the fuck up." Impotent rage piled on top of self-doubt. The second Olivia and I were out somewhere and we ran into another one of my former clients, would she fucking bolt? I strode back into the kitchen. Three pairs of eyes watched me from their beds in the living room like they knew to stay away.

"I know exactly what I'm talking about. If you pulled your head out of your ass, you would too. Take a week, fuck, take two, ride the fucking wave, but don't drown in it."

Anger, sharp and focused, took direct aim. "I'm not you. Two weeks is nothing."

The laugh he snorted out was bitter and well earned. "Doesn't mean the piece of ass in your bed gives a fuck about you long-term." He hung up.

My fist connected with the wall.

My forehead followed and pain throbbed in my knuckles.

Real wasn't this. It wasn't a fucking pipe dream of a tight cunt and a smart mouth twenty-four seven. What did I think would happen the second we walked outside these walls and my cock wasn't front and center in her universe? That she'd want a fucking hustler by her side, raising money for her charity?

"Hey." Soft and hesitant, it was the voice that'd said my name in the middle of the night.

I sucked in a breath and ignored my fucking knuckles. "Coffee?" I threw a mug under the machine.

"What's wrong?" The two smaller dogs trotted up beside her.

"Nothing." I briskly kissed her forehead and went to the fridge. The power had only been off twelve hours, shit was still cold. "Milk?"

She didn't answer.

I grabbed the carton. "I don't have cream, I have milk."

She stared at me.

I held the carton up. "Liv?"

The second her face paled I knew why.

Goddamn it. Two weeks was a fucking pipe dream. I hated Jared. I hated myself for letting him get in my head. "It's a nickname." Pissed at myself, there wasn't an ounce of apology in my tone.

"I'm going to shower." Her quiet, small voice said exactly what her words didn't.

Self-destructive, testing her, I drove it home. "I can't call you that?"

She paused long enough to look at me with hurt in her eyes. "It's not that you can't call me that. It's that you don't call me that." She walked away.

I picked up my phone and sent Jared my schedule and contacts—for the next two weeks.

THIRTY

Olivia

I WANTED TO CRY.

Water cascaded down my sore body and all the words that had tumbled from his lips last night played in a loop in my mind to torture me. *You're so goddamn beautiful. I wanna be inside you forever.*

Using his soap and his shampoo, I couldn't even wash the scent of him off me. The more I scrubbed, the more I smelled like him. I was a fool. I never should've let myself believe this would work out.

I didn't know who'd called, but it'd changed everything. Our hurricane bubble wasn't going to last forever, I knew that, but I didn't think a single phone call would turn everything around before the outer bands of the storm had even passed.

And that's why I was a fool. What did I think would happen when one of his *clients* called? That he'd ignore them because I was enough to satisfy him?

My heart crushed in on itself and I told myself I deserved it. I wasn't the girl who got to fall in love and live happily ever after. I was the girl who let her brother die and who shit all over her best friend. Miserable, I shut off the water and stepped out of the shower, but then I froze.

His arms crossed, his fitted boxers showing off exactly what he was made of, Alex leaned against the vanity. "I didn't know how you took your coffee." He nodded at the mug on the counter. "I put milk in it."

Self-conscious, I wrapped a towel around myself. "So that made you angry and distant?"

He watched my movements with the same hunger in his eyes as last night, but now there was something else. Sadness, regret, resolve, I didn't know what it was.

He pushed off the counter and took two strides. His knuckle tipped my chin and his lips met mine once. "No distance." His chaste kiss covered my lips one more time. "No anger."

I didn't want to ask what happened. I wanted to undo that phone call and live in our bubble forever. "Okay."

Merry nudged the bathroom door open wider and pushed her way in. She danced around Alex's feet until he glanced down at her and shook his head.

A tension-filled giggle escaped. "I'll get dressed and take her out."

Alex sighed. "She just wants my attention. I took her out a few hours ago."

"You did?" I didn't even hear him get up.

"Yeah, the little bitch jumped on the bed and licked at my face until I caved."

I laughed. I couldn't help it. The vision of a ten-pound terrier getting the best of a man Alex's size was priceless. "Well, she thinks she's your bitch now."

He bent and picked her up with one hand. Frowning, he chided her. "You're a pain in the ass, you know that?"

She kissed him.

Alex looked at me like he was totally put out. "She in fucking heat or something?"

I smiled. "She's claimed you."

Merry wiggled her tail in confirmation. Alex cursed. "Get dressed. We'll get food for the dogs then go check out your place."

My smile faltered, but I told myself he wasn't trying to get rid of me. "You don't happen to have a hair dryer, do you?"

He shook his head again, but he kissed my temple. "Bachelor pad, babe."

"Babe?"

"Christ." He growled. "Get dressed, woman, before I decide to spank you into submission."

My nipples hardened and my pussy tingled. "You wish," I teased.

His gaze dropped to my tits then between my legs. "You're right."

Instant heat that had nothing to do with the shower I'd just taken filled the bathroom. I was wondering exactly what spanking me into submission would entail when my phone buzzed. We both glanced at the display. Jesse.

I tightened the towel around me as it buzzed again.

"You gonna get that?"

I didn't want to answer it. "My hands are wet," I lied.

Alex picked my phone up and answered. "What's up?"

I bit my lip.

"It's Vega. She's indisposed…. She's fine. The dogs and her rode it out…. How bad?… Anything salvageable?… I'll handle it." His eyes trained on some distant point past me, Alex scowled. "I told you, I'll handle it…. You wanna know why I'm not gonna have this conversation with you? Because you fucked up."

I reached for my phone.

Alex leaned back. "That's the difference between you and me. I wouldn't have left her."

I heard Jesse yell through the line. "*Put her on the phone right now.*"

Alex handed the phone to me.

"Jesse."

His voice immediately softened. "You okay?"

"Fine. How'd your place do?" This didn't feel right. Niceties with my best friend in front of my... what? I didn't even know what Alex was.

"I'm good, but Liv, your place didn't do well."

My breath caught and my heart sank. "What do you mean? You've seen it?"

"I've been out checking on the buildings. I drove past your place. Liv, you're not going to be able to stay there."

I gripped the edge of the vanity. "What happened?"

"The roof's half gone. I already talked to your landlord. He'll reimburse your last rent payment, and he's gonna get it fixed, but until then...." He paused. "You can stay at my place."

I wanted to vomit. "What about all my stuff?"

"Everything except the furniture should be fine."

Oh God. I couldn't look at Alex. Tears welled.

As if Jesse knew I was falling apart, his voice softened. "Do you need me to come get you?"

Despair hovered. Like it'd hovered since the moment Alex's touch had bent everything I'd ever believed in. "Like you came to get me last night?"

Jesse exhaled. "I have a job to do, Liv. You know that."

I didn't know why I was lashing out at him. I wasn't even pissed about that. I could find a new apartment. I could wash my clothes. I hated my couch anyway. I strung all the reasons together and sucked in a breath. I wasn't going to fall apart. I was in one piece and the dogs were fine, that was all that mattered. That and not falling apart in front of Alex.

I toed a grout line on the cold tile floor and felt Alex's eyes on me like I felt the first chill of winter. The air was charged with coldness but tempered by humidity as it crawled across my skin and left my nerves tight.

"I'll come get you right now and we can get your stuff out of your place. If you don't want to stay with me, you can take one of the NC condos until you figure it out."

It struck me with such clarity, I was shocked I'd never seen it before. Jesse didn't want me, not really. He was driven by guilt because of my brother. "I don't blame you," I blurted.

Silence.

"Jesse?"

"Thank you." Simple and clean, he said it as if he'd been waiting for it.

I'd been waiting for it. "I never told you that. I thought I should—"

"Liv, it's okay. I get it."

"Thanks." Nothing moved, but my world shifted, and I felt Jesse slip away as surely as the hand that reached out and grasped my fingers gave me warmth. "Thanks for the offer of help, but I'm good. I'll figure out the apartment thing. I have to go."

"Liv, wait."

I hung up. I wasn't sad. I could breathe. My lungs filled,

my shoulders rose, the hurricane passed. Was this what forgiveness felt like?

I set my phone down.

Alex tightened his grip on my hand. "You okay?"

It struck me that there wasn't much of a difference between forgiveness and acceptance. One meant you let go and one meant you lived with the hand you were dealt. I stared at Alex and the pieces clicked into place. "The women, it wasn't really about the money, was it?" He'd come home from war changed but he'd accepted that difference and found a way to deal until he didn't need that anymore. He'd said he wasn't giving up his clients for me. He'd said he didn't need them anymore.

His gaze steady, he didn't blink. "Getting paid to have sex is its own kind of high."

My heart sank. "Do you need it, that high?"

He didn't hesitate. "No."

How was I supposed to trust that? "Why?"

His chest rose and fell twice, then his expression shut down. "It was also about distance."

"From what?" I asked, but I thought I already knew the answer. My brother had wanted distance.

"I didn't want to feel." Measured and guarded, the words were spoken without emotion. "The lifestyle, the women, I could control it." He searched my face. "I didn't have to feel."

"And now?" I barely whispered.

"It's different."

Air filled my lungs and a crushing weight lifted off my chest as hope filled my heart. "Because of me?"

Clipped, he nodded once. "Because of you."

"Will you always tell me the truth?

THRUST

"Yes." He glanced at my phone. "You done with him?"

"I was never with him."

"Not what I asked."

I was crazy. He was crazy. This conversation was crazy, and I didn't care. My world fit better with him in it, so I leapt. "He doesn't have my heart."

"No one's ever had mine." He stepped closer and the expressionless mask dropped as the corner of his mouth tipped up. "Until a smart-mouthed brunette threw a bottle of vodka at me."

"I was aiming for your head," I admitted.

"Your aim sucks."

I fake sighed. "I know."

He turned serious again. "You're staying with me."

I opened my mouth to protest and his lips landed on mine.

THIRTY-ONE

Alex

IT WAS THE BEST TWO WEEKS OF MY LIFE.

We fucked.

We laughed.

She gave me her trust.

I smiled at her as Charlie limped into the elevator behind me. The leash still in one hand, I took her into my arms and caged her in. My breath in her ear, my words coming from a place I never knew existed, I whispered, "Do you know what I'm going to do to you the second we get upstairs?"

Charlie's tail thumped against our legs.

She giggled. "Nothing if you don't remember to push the button."

I'd been so distracted by her sexy ass, I'd forgotten. With a cocky grin, I hit the penthouse key. "You like it when I push your buttons."

"You're right."

She smiled like she was happy, and it made me fucking happy. I cupped her face, but when I leaned in for a kiss, Charlie nudged me, hard.

Olivia fought a laugh. "Charlie, *sit*."

I stoked her cheek. "You really think he's gonna be

someone else's service dog?" She'd started training him the second he was back on his feet. She was gentle but firm with him and he responded to her. Just like me, he was a total goner for her. "He's got eyes for only one owner, sweetness."

She scratched his head. "He'll adapt."

"Why not keep him?" The three dogs had become more of a family than I'd ever had.

A half smile tipped her lips, but it didn't reach her eyes. "The roof is almost fixed at my apartment. I can't have dogs there."

The elevator doors opened and I silently let us into the penthouse. Even though I'd given her the code, she'd never used it. She still acted like a guest in my place. She didn't leave anything out on the counter in the bathroom. She kept her clothes neatly folded in her one suitcase. She never left a dish in the sink or so much as a sock in the dryer. It was as if she was waiting to leave.

And I was waiting to tell her what I'd done.

I exhaled as we stepped into the entry hall. "Olivia."

Sparks and Merry bounded up to us and demanded attention.

"Go lie down," I commanded.

All three dogs went to their beds as Olivia looked up at me in surprise. "They just wanted to say hi."

I took her arm and led her to the couch. Then I pulled her onto my lap. "I bought something."

She stiffened. "What kind of something."

I spit it out. "Land."

Air whooshed out of her lungs. "Okay."

My eyes narrowed. "What would have been the wrong answer?" I knew exactly what it would have been.

Her hand landed on my chest. "Nothing. What land?" She smiled sweetly.

It was fake. "You worried I bought you something else?"

"What?" She blinked in surprise. "No. I was just... I didn't know what you were going to say."

I fucking threw it out there because now I was irritated. "You thought I was going to say a ring."

"No." She adamantly shook her head. "I totally knew you wouldn't do that."

What the fuck? "Why not?"

Taking a deep breath, she tried to get off my lap, but I held her in place.

"Alex, it's been two weeks."

Two weeks, two months, two years, I didn't need another fucking second. I knew what this girl was the second I first sank inside her. "And?"

"You can't be serious. We're going to have this conversation?"

Dead serious. "We're already having it."

"No, you said you bought land. We were talking about that."

"Why the fuck do you think I did that? You think I'm playing house?"

Anger tinted her cheeks and her tone. "I don't know what you're doing." She pushed off my lap and made it one step.

I grabbed her hand and told myself to let her go, but I was already on my feet. "You know what I want. I've never hidden that from you." I'd told her every night as I sank inside her that she was mine.

She spun and the tears in her voice crushed my heart,

but when she spoke, she crushed my hope. "You didn't even give us two weeks!"

My thoughts fractured.

Thirteen days since the hurricane. One day short of two weeks. I'd been so deep into Olivia, my schedule still sat on my phone. My contacts still listed. I'd forgotten to pass the rest of it off to Jared. I'd walked away from that old life without once looking back. Mission intent, I'd bought land. I'd hired Neil. I'd made a plan. Olivia was my world. She was *all* of that plan. But she knew. She knew about the two weeks.

How did she fucking know?

"I heard you," she accused, answering my silent question. "I heard you on the phone the morning after the hurricane."

Premature relief flooded my veins, and I smiled. "I wasn't giving us two weeks." That was all Jared. "You thought we had an expiration date?"

"You said you could do two weeks."

Inappropriately, and with shit timing, I laughed. "I can do a hell of a lot more than two weeks with you, sweetness." I pulled her into my arms. "Come here."

"This isn't funny." She melted into me anyway.

I pulled back just enough to grasp her chin. "You're right, it's not. You should have said something to me. I told you what I wanted. I told you I wasn't playing games. I thought you understood."

"I barely know you, Alex," she quietly admitted.

"You know me better than anyone else." Simply truth. I let no one in. Ever. But I wanted to let her in, so I told her what I'd done. "I bought land and hired Neil to build a training facility and kennel. There'll also be grooming facilities. If I thought you'd accept it, I would've bought a ring too."

Her eyes went wide and her mouth formed an O.

"Which part is shocking you?"

She blinked, then blinked again and fought tears welling. "You bought a place to train dogs?"

I fought a smile and shook my head. Of course it was about the dogs. It was always about the dogs for her, but I couldn't be pissed because the truth was, I wouldn't want her any other way. She was fucking perfect. "I bought a place for *you* to train dogs," I corrected.

"Why?"

I stared at the most beautiful woman I'd ever laid eyes on and I told her what I'd wanted to say since the first time I'd held her in my arms. "Because I love you."

The tears fell.

Shit. "Olivia." My thumbs swept across her cheeks.

"No, no, it's good. I'm fine. I mean, I love you too." Her eyes shining with joy, she laughed. "I'm just, *oh my God.*" She laughed again as she pushed my hands away and brushed at her face. Then she tried and failed to look serious. "I might've fallen for you the second you said you could make me come twice with ice cubes."

My head fell back and I laughed my fucking ass off. "You little vixen, it's all about the sex to you, isn't it?"

She grinned. "Yes?"

"Thank Christ." I kissed her.

"Wait." She pulled back. "So, um, is that even possible?"

I stripped her clothes off and showed her exactly how possible it was.

EPILOGUE

Olivia

"**W**ALK," HE WARNED.

I smiled because I knew that tone. "Where?" My nipples hardened.

He scanned the length of my body, calculating and slow. "You know where."

I took a step backward. He was so fucking sexy, I was already wet.

"Pants off," he demanded.

I loved him bossy. But as much as I wanted to, I never gave in too easily. I hooked a thumb in my waistband. "These pants?"

His nostrils flared on an inhale and his eyes dropped to the juncture of my legs. "Now."

I took my shirt off and smiled sweetly.

He rushed me.

I was over his shoulder and he'd spanked my ass before I could draw a breath. Girlie and totally not sexy, I squealed. It netted me another slap and desire soaked my underwear. "Do that again and you'll be sorry!" Except I didn't sound threatening, I sounded breathless and turned on.

He strode into our bedroom and threw me on the bed.

243

His giant hands hit my waist and he peeled my leggings off with one tug. "*Don't* move."

I grabbed my tits and pushed them together. "At all?"

"You touch my cunt, I'm not letting you come." He walked out.

"Hey!" He never left me alone and naked. "Where are you going?"

"No touching." He disappeared down the hall.

"It's my body," I yelled. "I'll touch myself if I want to!"

A kitchen cupboard door banged shut and a few seconds later the distinctive sound of ice hitting glass carried across the penthouse.

Oh shit.

I sat up and scooted back on the bed.

He strode into the bedroom shirtless. His stare intense, the corner of his mouth tipped up as he took a sip of whiskey from a tumbler full of ice.

Oh shit, oh shit, oh shit. "A little early, isn't it?" I admit, I'd wanted to know how the hell he'd thought he could make a woman come with ice cubes the second he'd said it that first night I met him. I'd maybe even fantasized about it. But now, being naked and seeing the condensation on that glass? I shoved my thighs together.

"Spread those legs, sweetness." Deep and commanding, his voice was liquid seduction.

Nope, nah-uh, no way. "Put the glass down."

Ignoring me, he took another sip.

My pulse kicked up a notch. "Put it across the room, or better yet, back in the kitchen, where it belongs."

He downed the rest of the whiskey in one swallow and set the glass on the bed. His biceps flexed and he was reaching

for me. Huge hands wrapped around my ankles and he effortlessly pulled me to the edge. Spreading my legs, he bent my
knees up and leaned over me. A hairsbreadth away from making contact just to drive me mad, he lowered his lips to mine.

Cold whiskey filled my mouth and dribbled down my
chin.

He whispered against ear. "Swallow."

The alcohol burned going down my throat, but then he
sank his tongue into my mouth and the taste of him and whiskey made me moan.

He expertly swept his tongue through my heat and I dug
my fingers into his dark hair. Soft and so damn thick, I grasped
two handfuls and tried to pull him to me as I wrapped my legs
around his hips.

"Ah, ah, ah." He pushed my knees out and leaned back.
With a glint in his eyes, he fished two ice cubes out of the glass
and popped them into his mouth.

Oh God. "I changed my—"

He crunched the cubes between his teeth, pushed my legs
wide, and his mouth landed on me.

Bits of ice and his searing-cold tongue swirled across my
clit and sank into my pussy. Gooseflesh raced across my skin
and my whole body convulsed in a shiver. My back arched
and my hands yanked his hair as I flew into a sitting position.
"*Holy shit.*"

He shoved my legs wider and icy cold water flowed from
his mouth into my pussy. Thrusting his tongue then biting my
clit, cold and heat and pleasure and pain spun into a frenzy. I
heard the clink of ice in the glass, but he drew my clit between
his teeth and my head fell back. Sucking, pressure, his tongue
working my clit, he pushed ice into my pussy.

My thighs jerked, his teeth drew down, and my muscles clenched.

Oh my God.

Oh my God.

I came so hard and fast, I screamed.

His fingers inside me, pushing the ice around, my legs shaking, his tongue warm and lapping on my clit, I had no words. My hands in his hair as my only anchor, I fell back on the bed.

Rough and scratchy, I pushed a sentence past my dry throat. "That was only once."

His low chuckle should have been a warning but I couldn't string two thoughts together. He pulled his fingers out and melted ice and the remnants of the cubes leaked out of me as I pulsed with aftershocks.

Going to his knees, he slid his hands under my thighs and dragged me up his legs. "Arms above your head," he commanded.

Without even a thought, I laced my fingers together and did as he said. Spread wide, my ass hovering just above the bed, I thought he would enter me.

But he didn't.

One torturous ice cube at a time, he drew slow circles over every inch of my sensitive flesh. Rimming my opening, pressing on my tender clit, he even dragged the ice over my nipples until they ached. "*Alex.*" Desire built faster than I could inhale, but the ice was so cold, I didn't know if I was begging him for more or pleading with him to stop.

Rhythmic and slow, he stroked himself. "I want more than a ring on your finger."

My gaze cut to his. Fierce, intent, the look in his eyes

made my heart skip. "What?" The last ice cube melted and dripped down between my cheeks.

His cock circled my entrance. "I want it all." He shoved all the way home.

The heat of his intrusion in my ice-cooled flesh exploded into fire and desire. "*Ahhhhh.*"

Stroking in and out, covering my body with his, caging me in with his strength, he brushed his lips against mine. "You, me, the dogs, kids, forever. I want it all with you."

My heart soaring, my body trembling for him, I begged. "Yes, please."

"Say my name."

"Alex, Alex, *Alex.*"

"You own me," he growled, thrusting hard.

Deep in my body, pressed against my womb, the first pulse of his release filled me with more than his heat. I wasn't a shattered heart and broken pieces. I was everything I ever wanted to be and it was because of him. "I love you."

His tongue sank into my mouth and I followed him over the edge.

THANK YOU!

Thank you so much for reading THRUST! If you were interested in leaving a review on any retail site, I would be so appreciative. Reviews mean the world to authors, and they are helpful beyond compare!

Have you read the other books in the Alpha Escort Series?
ROUGH—Jared's story
GRIND—Dane's story

Have you met the Alpha heroes in the Uncompromising Series?
TALON
NEIL
ANDRÉ
BENNETT
CALLAN

And check out the new Alpha Bodyguard Series!
SCANDALOUS – Tank's Story
MERCILESS – Collins's Story
RECKLESS – Tyler's Story
RUTHLESS – Sawyer's Story
FEARLESS – Ty's Story
CALLOUS – Preston's Story
RELENTLESS – Thomas's story

Turn the page for a preview of ROUGH,
the next book in the sexy Alpha Escort Series!

Join Sybil Bartel's Mailing List to get the news first on the next books in this series and to hear about her other upcoming releases, giveaways and exclusive excerpts. You'll also get a FREE book for joining!

ROUGH

THE ALPHA ESCORT SERIES

Jared

I'm not your boyfriend. I'm not the guy next door. I don't even play nice.

My hands twisting in your hair, my whispered demand in your ear—I'm the fantasy you wish you never had.

When I'm through with you, every inch of your body will know where I've been. You won't crave more, you'll beg for it, because I'm not just the cocky smile with military-hardened muscles you paid for—I'm the experience you'll never forget.

One night with me and you'll know exactly why women pay me to be rough.

ACKNOWLEDGMENTS

There are so many moving parts and pieces to writing a book that there is no way I could do this alone. The first thing you see when you look at book is the cover and I always have an idea in my head before I even write the book. Somehow, someway, Clarise at CT Cover Creations is always able to make those visions a reality. She is a cover artist ninja! Thank you, Clarise!

Every book needs editors and great editors make all the difference! I am so lucky to have Virginia and Olivia from Hot Tree Edits in my corner, making my words pretty and my grammar better. And they still put up with me even though I have no idea what the difference is between sank and sunk, LOL! Thank you, Virginia and Olivia!

Formatting. The word alone used to make me twitch but Stacy at Champagne Formats is so amazing, she creates magic! Thank you, Stacy!

THRUST had two special people that helped make this book a reality. My amazing friend and fellow author Elizabeth Briggs listened to and encouraged me to go for it with this book. She put up with my countless questions and hesitations and I am so grateful for her wisdom and friendship because she is awesome! And Kristen, beta reader extraordinaire, took my words, last-minute and a week late and dropped everything to read this story for me. Her advice smoothed out the rough edges and I am so thankful for her help. Thank you, Kristen! One day, we're going to eat that pizza together!

And to my readers… I have no words except you all humble me with your support. I am so grateful and I could not do this without you! Thank you for making my dreams come true and for reading all my words. XOXO

ABOUT THE AUTHOR

Sybil Bartel grew up in northern California with her head in a book and her feet in the sand. Trading one coast for another, she now resides in Southern Florida. When Sybil isn't writing or fighting to contain the banana plantation in her backyard, you can find her spending time with her handsomely tattooed husband, her brilliantly practical son and a mischievous miniature boxer...

But Seriously?

Here are ten things you probably really want to know about Sybil.

She grew up a faculty brat. She can swear like a sailor. She loves men in uniform. She hates being told what to do. She can do your taxes (but don't ask). The Bird Market in Hong Kong scares her. Her favorite word has four letters. She has a thing for muscle cars. But never rely on her for driving directions, ever. And she has a new book boyfriend every week.

To find out more about Sybil Bartel or her books, please visit her at:

Website: www.sybilbartel.com

Facebook page: www.facebook.com/sybilbartelauthor

Book Boyfriend Heroes:
www.facebook.com/groups/1065006266850790/

Twitter: twitter.com/SybilBartel

BookBub: www.bookbub.com/authors/sybil-bartel

Newsletter: http://eepurl.com/bRSE2T

Made in United States
Troutdale, OR
12/23/2023

16385589R00146